WITCH'S OATH

TERRY GOODKIND is a number one *New York Times* bestselling author. His Sword of Truth series has sold over 20 million copies. Before writing full-time, Terry worked as a wildlife artist, a cabinetmaker and a violin maker. He writes thrillers as well as epic fantasy and lives in the desert in Nevada.

BY TERRY GOODKIND

THE SWORD OF TRUTH SERIES

Wizard's First Rule
Stone of Tears
Blood of the Fold
Temple of the Winds
Soul of the Fire
Faith of the Fallen
The Pillars of Creation
Naked Empire
Debt of Bones
Chainfire
Phantom
Confessor
The Omen Machine
The First Confessor
The Third Kingdom
Severed Souls
Warheart

THE CHILDREN OF D'HARA

The Scribbly Man
Hateful Things
Wasteland
Witch's Oath
Into Darkness (March 2020)

THE NICCI CHRONICLES

Death's Mistress
Shroud of Eternity
Siege of Stone

THE ANGELA CONSTANTINE SERIES

Trouble's Child
The Girl in the Moon
Crazy Wanda

The Law of Nines
Nest

TERRY GOODKIND

WITCH'S OATH

A Children of D'Hara Novella

Episode 4

First published by Head of Zeus in 2020

This is a work of fiction. All characters, organizations, and events portrayed in this novel are either products of the author's imagination or are used fictitiously.

9 7 5 3 1 2 4 6 8

A catalogue record for this book is available from the British Library.

ISBN (HB): 9781789541311
ISBN (E): 9781789541304

Printed and bound by
CPI Group (UK) Ltd, Croydon, CR0 4YY

Head of Zeus Ltd
First Floor East
5–8 Hardwick Street
London EC1R 4RG
WWW.HEADOFZEUS.COM

WITCH'S OATH

1

Kahlan's scream not only felt as if it ripped Richard's soul, it overwhelmed him with shock and terror. He couldn't understand or remember how he had come to be hanging in a room full of skinned corpses also hanging by their wrists from the ceiling, but he realized it had to be a spell of some sort cast by the witch man, Moravaska Michec. More than that, what had happened or how it had happened didn't really matter. All that mattered was what was, now.

A quick glance to his left showed Shale, manacles around her wrists, likewise hanging on a chain attached to the ceiling and facing in the same direction he was. She appeared to be unconscious and so could be of no help.

The same distance to his right and facing in the same direction, toward all the hanging corpses, Kahlan struggled in panic at what was happening, at what was about to happen. The smell of all the dead bodies hanging in a grid pattern throughout the room was not only sickening, it was overpowering.

Despite how much Kahlan thrashed around, making her wrists bleed all the more as the manacles cut into her flesh, Michec had a firm grip on her flesh, with his fat thumb on the outside and two fingers in under the slit he had cut in the skin at the side of her throat so that he could begin skinning her alive.

Richard clearly remembered Michec saying he had spelled the room to block their gift. That had to be the reason she hadn't used her power on him. The thought of Moravaska Michec skinning Kahlan alive was more than Richard could take. He tried to reach his own gift, but when he did, it felt as if nothing was there. He simply felt empty.

As long as Michec's spell blocked their gift, his gift could be of no help.

Directly across from Richard, Vika, as naked as Kahlan, hung helpless in manacles facing him. Despite the agony she was in from the gash Michec had made in her abdomen to pull out a length of her intestines, and the Agiel he had pushed into the open wound to increase the torture, she was clearly distraught watching Kahlan in the clutches of that evil man. A man who had once owned Vika.

"Master," Vika called out in a weak voice, but a voice that Michec heard.

Annoyed, he turned a frown back over his shoulder at her, expecting to know why she would interrupt him.

"Master," Vika managed again in a shaky voice.

"What!" he shouted in anger at being interrupted before he could begin skinning Kahlan alive.

"I'm trying to warn you. You've made a terrible mistake."

The witch man's expression darkened, but curiosity caused him to take a step back from Kahlan. He wiped his bloody fingers on his filthy robes as he turned toward Vika. His blocky features were tight with displeasure at being called away from what he was so eager to do to Kahlan.

Richard sagged in the manacles with relief that Vika had managed to stop him, if only for a moment, from what he had been about to do. Kahlan sagged as she watched, fearing his return.

Michec moved closer so that he could hear Vika's weak voice. "Warn me about what?"

"Master, it is my duty to tell you that you have made a dangerous mistake."

"What mistake?" When she failed to answer immediately, he pushed her Agiel in a little deeper, making her gasp as her head tipped back in agony. "What mistake!"

Richard could see the muscles in her legs tense. She clenched her teeth and held her breath for a moment, doing her best to endure the increase in agony caused by her Agiel.

Panting to get her breath, Vika finally brought her head back down. "The same mistake made by Darken Rahl. The same mistake made by Hannis Arc. The same mistake made by Emperor Sulachan. The same mistake made by so many others."

Moravaska Michec, angry to be told he was making a mistake of any kind, stepped close and grabbed her Agiel. He twisted it back and forth, sweeping it around inside the wound in her belly, making her cry out involuntarily as her eyes rolled up in her head with the pain, unable to endure it, yet unable to do anything to stop it. Her legs trembled; her feet shook. Richard ached at seeing how helpless she was.

Michee released the Agiel and gripped one of the ropy braids of his beard between a dirty finger and thumb. One brow arched over a dark, angry eye. "What mistake would that be?"

Her muscles stood out iron hard from the torment of the Agiel jutting from the open wound. She finally managed to gasp in enough air to speak. She stared at him with wet, sky-blue eyes. "The mistake . . . of underestimating Lord Rahl."

Michee gestured irritably toward Richard. "Him? He is not worthy to be called Lord Rahl."

"Call him what you will. Call him a mere woodsman if you will. But it is my duty to warn you, Master, that you have made a fatal mistake."

"First, I underestimated him, and now I've made a fatal mistake?"

Her jaw trembling in pain, tears running down her cheeks, Vika nodded.

Michec's brow drew down over his cruel eyes. His arm lifted in a grand gesture. "And what fatal mistake do you imagine I've made?"

Vika had to pause to swallow back her agony. "You did not kill him when you had the chance. Richard Rahl does not make the mistake of trying to teach his enemies lessons. He does not keep them alive to lecture them and gloat. He simply kills them."

Even though Vika was advising Michec to kill him, Richard had faith that she was doing it for good reason. He realized it was a distraction to make Michec stop before it was too late and he started skinning Kahlan alive, even though it meant he would turn his formidable wrath on her. Richard feared for Vika but was beyond grateful for her intervention.

When he saw movement out of the corner of his eye, a quick glance revealed that Shale was at last awake. In that quick glance they shared, they both knew the despair of their situation.

Michec stared at the Mord-Sith briefly, as if considering her words, or possibly what more painful torture he could inflict, then huffed a brief chuckle. The snakelike braids of his beard swung around with him as he turned and stared at Richard a moment. The greasy spikes of salt-and-pepper hair stood out against the pale greenish light from the glass spheres around the room. Michee flicked a hand dismissively toward Richard as he looked back at Vika.

"I appreciate your loyalty in trying to warn me of danger, but you underestimate me. The famous and powerful Lord Rahl is quite helpless against me. No one escapes a witch's oath."

"He is gifted. I have seen him kill with his gift."

Michee's derisive smile distorted his coarse features. "Gifted? I've blocked his gift"—he thumped a fist against his own puffed-up chest—"the same as I blocked your ability to use your Agiel against me, and I blocked the ability of the other Mord-Sith, and I blocked this witch woman's gift, and I blocked the Mother Confessor's power. No one but me can use their power in this room. So, you see? You are quite wrong. He is hardly a danger to me, now. His questionable 'powers' won't help him. He is under the decree of a witch's oath."

"I am telling you, Master, you have made a fatal mistake. You arrogantly think to give him a show of your superiority, and in that arrogance, you have let your chance to kill him slip away. You will not get another chance."

Michec turned a look of raw hatred toward Richard. He slowly closed the distance from Vika, his glare fixed on Richard the whole time. He paused briefly to glance once over at Kahlan with lust for what was being delayed. She glared back with loathing and defiance. He smiled, pleased by that look. He finally came to a stop before Richard to look up at his helpless prize.

"Dangerous, are you?" He planted his fists on his hips as he glared up at Richard with contempt. "Then maybe I should take the advice of my loyal Mord-Sith, and—"

As hard as he could, Richard kicked the witch man in the face. His boot connected with bone. Richard didn't know if it was skull or jawbone, but Michec's dead weight toppled back. He landed hard on his back and lay motionless, sprawled on the floor, his arms out to the side. He looked to be out cold.

Her brow bunching with the effort, Vika flashed Richard a shaky smile through her pain. "I bought you time. Now get out of here."

"Richard . . ." Kahlan said.

He looked where she was looking and saw the dark shapes of the Glee cautiously stepping out of the shadows of the hanging, skinless corpses. Like those corpses, Richard also hung helpless from manacles around his wrists. Those creatures would not wait for Michee to come around and finally finish his work with Kahlan so they could have her.

He knew they would take the opportunity to have what they had come for—the babies in Kahlan's womb.

2

Richard looked from the dark, glistening shapes of the cautious Glee back in among the shadows and hanging corpses to the unconscious form sprawled on the floor in front of him. Had he been able to brace against something solid when he kicked Michec in the head he might have been able to kill him. Hanging helpless, he had done the best he could. At the least, the big man was out cold for the moment.

Richard knew he had only a small window of time before either Michec came around or the Glee decided that this was their opportunity to take what they wanted.

Richard pressed his knees together and lifted his legs out in front of him, then let them fall back. He did it several more times to get his whole body to start swinging back and forth, each time pumping his legs to get each arcing movement higher and higher. The chain grated in protest as the top link pivoted from the fat eyebolt in the ceiling. Once he was swinging back and forth as much as he could, he threw his legs around to his right and kept contorting his body, changing that pendulum motion to rotation. As he swung his legs, he twisted his whole body around, swinging faster and faster, building momentum.

Once all the slack was gone out of the chain as he continued to turn it with his body, the links couldn't resist the strain and they started folding over on top of one another. The more he spun, the more it twisted the chain and the harder it was to keep the rotation going. As he spun the chain, it continually increased the pressure of the manacles on his wrists. They cut painfully into the flesh. He gripped the chain above the manacles to try to take some of the pressure off his wrists as he spun. Richard ignored the pain and kept swinging his legs around and around to force the chain to turn, hoping something would have to give way.

As he did, the links continued to bunch and knot up.

Suddenly, the pressure was too much, and the eyebolt in the ceiling beam let out a snapping sound as the rusty threads finally broke their bond to the wood. With the threads broken free, the twisting force caused the bolt to begin to turn, unscrewing it from the wooden beam. The age and corrosion of the threads caused them to want to bind up and made it difficult to keep up the turning force. Despite the difficulty, Richard knew he couldn't stop, or he might never get it going again. He kept swinging his legs around and around to keep the eyebolt unscrewing. He didn't dare rest for fear it would bind up and stick.

Although Michec still lay unconscious on the floor, Richard knew the man could come around at any moment. But right then there was a bigger concern. With each rotation he could see the Glee advancing across the room to get to Kahlan. He knew that with one powerful swipe of their claws they could rip her open. By Kahlan's rapid breathing, he knew she was well aware of that imminent threat.

All of a sudden, the turning eyebolt broke

free of the beam. Richard crashed to the floor. He quickly scrambled to his feet as several of the dark shapes were going for Kahlan.

He grabbed the heavy chain in both hands and started swinging it around over his head. The first two Glee saw that he was now free and a threat, so they turned away from Kahlan toward him, eager to attack. Richard whipped the chain around and cracked it against the side of the head of one of them. The big eyebolt at the end of the chain split its skull and sent the creature sprawling.

Before the second could get to him, he swung the chain again. Because the second Glee raced in closer, he couldn't hit it in the head with the eyebolt at the end of the chain. Instead, the chain caught the side of its neck. The heavy eyebolt and the rest of the chain continued their flight, and the chain wrapped twice around the creature's neck. Richard immediately yanked the chain before the Glee could grab it or get its balance. The force of that pull twisted its head around, breaking its neck. Like the first one, the second fell dead before being able to vanish.

Suddenly there were more Glee coming for

both him and Kahlan. He shortened his grip on the chain and stood far enough in front of her that he wouldn't accidentally hit her as he continued swinging it around. The speed of the heavy chain was deadly. He took down the Glee as fast as they could come.

"Shale!" Kahlan yelled. "Do something to help him!"

"My gift doesn't work any more than yours does," the sorceress called back. "Don't you remember? Michec blocked our power in this room."

Richard knew there would be no help coming. It was all up to him to stop the threat or Kahlan would die. They all would die.

As masses of the Glee converged and all came for him, he threw himself into the battle. He kept the chain spinning overhead fast as he could, whipping it against the creatures as soon as they were close enough. The eyebolt at the end of the chain whistled as it swept through the air. Almost as fast as he downed one and another got close enough, he cracked the heavy eyebolt against its skull. Most slowed and stayed back out of range. Others came for him, thinking they could duck under and evade the chain. He saw sharp white teeth snapping at his face. He caught the chain and doubled it over so he could swing it at them like a bat. That doubled the weight of each impact.

As he was fighting off a number of Glee at the same time, one of them somehow suddenly got in close. Before it could claw him or bite his face, Richard threw a loop of the chain over its head and around its neck. He put his knee between the thing's shoulder blades and hauled back on the chain, letting out a yell with the effort until he felt and heard the windpipe crush in. Once it did, he kicked another of the tall, dark creatures back and immediately hit it in the head with the doubled-over chain.

Richard lost himself in a world of seemingly endless, bloody battle. The rhythm of what he was doing soon became what he knew so well. It became the dance with death.

He killed the creatures as fast as they could come at him. Those that were severely injured and were able vanished back into their world. The air in Richard's world was filled with howls and shrieks of the enraged creatures and of the wounded and dying. The floor was slick with blood and slime of the dead.

Panting from the effort, Richard paused, looked around for more of the enemy, more targets. He suddenly realized that there were no more Glee still standing. A number of them lay dead, many sprawled over the top of others. The last of the howls and shrieks still seemed to echo in his head.

He raced back to the witch man to strangle him with the chain before he could wake up.

Michec was gone.

3

Richard quickly looked around, hoping to be able to find and catch Michec before he could get away, but he was nowhere to be seen. He gritted his teeth in rage that the witch man was no longer there on the floor. He had to kill the man before he could do anything else to them—before he could kill them first.

"Did you see where he went?" he asked Kahlan and Shale.

Both shook their heads.

Before doing anything else, Richard rushed to Vika and yanked the Agiel from the gaping wound in her belly. She gasped. Holding the Agiel sent a jolt of pain up through his elbow, making him flinch. The blow of pain felt as if he had been hit in the back of the skull with an iron bar. It made his ears ring. He could not imagine the agony of having that weapon jammed inside an open wound.

He tossed the Agiel on the floor, then touched her bloody, trembling leg as he looked up into her wet eyes. "Hold on, Vika."

"Kill me," she pleaded. "Please, Lord Rahl. There is no hope for me now. Please, end it."

"Just hold on," he said. "I'm going to help you. Trust me."

Angry that he couldn't kill Michec right then and there, he dragged the heavy chain attached to his manacles over to his sword and baldric, which lay under where he had been hanging. He had to grab the arm of one of the dark, slimy creatures lying over the bottom half of the scabbard and flip it over and off the weapon. He started to pull the sword out of the scabbard with his hands, but because they were chained closely together, he had to hold the scabbard between his boots to be able to draw the blade the rest of the way out.

A familiar sensation stormed through him. He felt a fool.

With the hilt held in both hands, it was with great relief that he felt the anger of the sword's magic join his to blossom into full rage. He immediately turned and swung the sword over the sorceress's head. Sparks flew as the blade shattered the iron chain and sent links flying. Shale dropped to the floor.

"Hold your hands out," he told her.

When she did, and she saw what he was about to do and that she didn't have enough time to stop him, she gasped in fear as she turned her face away. The blade whistled through the air as it came down in an arc and hit the manacles with a glancing blow to the side of her wrists. It was enough to shatter the metal bands. Shards of hot steel skittered across the room bouncing along the rough stone floor.

Shale, somewhat surprised to still have her hands, was relieved to finally have the horrible devices off. She rubbed her bleeding wrists.

"Hold Kahlan for me," he told the sorceress before she had the chance to thank him.

Shale hugged her arms around Kahlan's legs to lift her weight a little. As soon as she did, Richard took a mighty swing at the chain holding Kahlan up by her wrists. The iron links blew apart when hit with the singular blade, as if made of nothing more than clay. Hot, broken bits of chain sailed off through the air.

Together Shale and Richard lowered Kahlan down to stand on the floor. She held her hands out as she turned her bruised and bleeding face away so Richard could break the manacles from around her wrists. In relief, once they were off, she threw her arms around his neck. Richard returned the hug as best he could with both of his wrists still in manacles, and while doing so let healing magic flow into her just long enough to ease her pain a little. The rest would have to wait.

When he released her to turn and look for any threat, she sank down to the floor in a squat, elbows in tight at her sides, holding her head in her hands, comforting the painful wounds Michec had inflicted but also thankful for at least the little healing Richard had done. He put a hand on her shoulder, relieved that she was safe, at least for the moment. Without looking up, Kahlan reached up to grip his hand a moment.

He understood the wordless meaning in that touch.

Then, with Shale's help holding the Mord-Sith's weight, Richard used his sword to break the chain holding her. As soon as he did, he immediately moved to help Shale carefully lower the Mord-Sith to the floor. Shale and Kahlan both held Vika's arms as he shattered the manacles around her wrists.

As the metal shards were still bouncing across the stone floor, a sound made him turn toward the back of the vast room.

There, in the distance beyond the hanging, skinless corpses, he saw the air come alive with masses of scribbles as hundreds of Glee began to materialize, pouring out of nowhere into a mad dash toward them. They went around and among the hanging dead like a raging river flooding around rocks on their way to Richard, Kahlan, Shale and Vika.

Without pause, still in the haze of rage from the sword, he turned to face the threat. Shale seized Kahlan in a protective hug, turning her own back to the danger.

Still lost in the dance with death from fighting the last onslaught of Glee, Richard acted without forethought.

He went to his right knee. Holding the sword in both hands, he thrust it out toward the mass of dark shapes coming for them, teeth clacking, claws reaching, as they screeched with murderous intent.

From somewhere deep within, his war-wizard birthright, his instinct, his raging need took over. That inheritance of power shot through his grip on the hilt, adding destructive force to the sword's rage. Light ignited from the tip of the sword. The room shook with a crack, as if the sword had been hit by lightning.

The horizontal wedge of light that flared from the tip of the sword came out razor thin and as sharp as his blade. The blindingly bright flash of flawless white illumination was so flat and thin as to be insubstantial, like a glowing pane of glass, yet at the same time it was pure menace.

Everything that razor-thin flare of light touched was instantly severed.

Corpses were sliced cleanly in half through bone and flesh as that flat blade of light effortlessly flared through them. The stiff bottom halves of the bodies thumped down to the floor.

That same wedge of light cut through the Glee like a hot knife through silk. There was no escaping the instantaneous, blindingly bright knife of light.

Dark, severed legs collapsed. The top halves of slimy torsos, arms still flailing, tumbled across the floor, spilling their insides as they crashed down. Some of the Glee clawed at the floor, trying to reach him. Since they were without legs and losing blood at a catastrophic rate, those efforts quickly died out as life left them. It all happened so fast that none of them managed to dive to the floor to evade the cutting light or vanish back into their home world.

The Golden Goddess would never hear from the attack force.

The instant that sheet of light ignited, everything before it was sliced in two. Almost as soon as it had ignited, the flat wedge of light extinguished. It had only lasted an instant, but that was all it had taken.

Even though the light was gone, the room still reverberated with the crack of thunder it had created. Slowly, even that sound died out, to leave the room in ringing silence. What looked like hundreds of Glee lay in a tangled, bleeding mass, a few arms still weakly clawing at the air. In another moment, even that residual muscle movement ceased, and the room went still as Richard, motionless on one knee, the manacles still around his wrists with the chain attached, head bowed, held the sword out toward the vanquished threat.

When he finally stood and turned back, he saw Shale standing stock-still in wide-eyed shock. Kahlan, who only a moment before had been bracing with the sorceress for the swift death about to descend upon them, let out a sigh as she sagged in relief.

4

"Richard," Shale finally whispered into the haunting silence, "how in the world did you just do that? For that matter, what in the world did you just do?"

Richard had no real answer. Truth be told, he was at a loss to understand what he had just done, much less explain it to her. He had simply acted out of instinct—a war wizard's instinct.

"I ended the threat," he said in simple explanation, without trying to embellish with guesses about what he couldn't explain.

"No . . . well, yes, but what I mean, is how could you possibly do that? That was clearly magic. Michec blocked us from using our magic in this room. For that matter, how did your sword work? Your sword shouldn't work in here either. You shouldn't be able to use your gift in here."

Richard arched an eyebrow at her. "And you believe that?"

"Of course." Her brow tightened. "I could feel that I couldn't use my gift. It was blocked. How were you able to use yours?"

"He's not a wizard, but he used Wizard's First Rule."

Her face twisted with bewilderment. "Wizard's what?"

Richard wet his lips. "I don't think that a witch man even as powerful as Michec could do something like block us from our gift. But you were afraid it was true, so you believed it. By believing it, in a way you made it true. You blocked your gift because in your own mind you believed a block was there. You expected to be blocked from your ability. I don't think Michec really has the ability to do such a thing. At least not to us. To the Mord-Sith, yes, because he was a trainer to Mord-Sith, but not us. Sometimes a trick is the best magic."

"But how did you know?"

Richard showed her a crooked smile. "A lesson my grandfather taught me. I just wish

I hadn't been so slow to remember the lesson and realize what was really happening. If I had realized that lesson sooner, I would have been able to kill Michec while still hanging from the chain.

"Without thinking, while I thought my gift was blocked, I expected the magic of the sword to work when I grabbed the hilt. When it did, I suddenly realized there couldn't be a block or I wouldn't be able to feel its power bonding with me. It was just a trick. I had been believing it because I was afraid it was true."

Shale shook her head. "I wish I had realized it. I could have done something."

"We all believed it because Michec is a scary character. That's how such a trick works. It has to be convincing. Michec is convincing, but he has limitations."

Richard turned to Kahlan and held her bloody face gently in his hands. He kissed her forehead, relieved beyond words that she was safe, at least for the moment. He hated to see all that blood on her face. He briefly released a flow of Subtractive Magic as he held her head between his hands, making the blood on her face vanish and easing a little more of her pain.

"Do you think you can hold on for a bit?" he whispered to her. "I need to help Vika."

Kahlan nodded. "Michec did no serious damage to me. Don't worry about me. You have to help Vika if you can."

As Richard turned, an astonished Shale hooked his arm. With her other hand she waggled a finger at Kahlan. "How did you make the blood on her face vanish?"

"Subtractive Magic. I told you. There is no block on our gift." He held both hands out, still in the manacles. "Now, show me I'm right by using your gift to get these off me."

Giving him a dark look, she opened her mouth to question him, but then put her hands around the manacles. She closed her eyes as she concentrated on the task. Richard heard a snap as the lock on the metal bands broke. He twisted his hands, and to his great relief the manacles with the chain still attached fell open and dropped to the floor.

"Thanks. See? Your gift was there all the time." He gestured toward the opening to the room off in the distance. "Now, keep a sharp lookout for Michec. He's out there somewhere and he is not going to so easily give up. I have to help Vika before he shows up again."

The sorceress tightened her grip on his arm. Her eyes reflected the pain of sympathy, and regret. She hesitated briefly, then leaned in close and spoke softly so that Vika wouldn't hear.

"Lord Rahl, her wounds are too grievous to heal. Healing is part of my ability, something I've done my whole life. I know what is possible and what is not possible. There is nothing that can be done for her. You must believe me that I know what I'm talking about. She cannot be healed of a gut wound that serious, to say nothing of what else he did to that poor girl.

"But beyond that, even if it were within the scope of the possible, a complex healing takes many hours. An extremely complex healing can take days. Michec is still down here, somewhere. He is not going to give up on a witch's oath. He will come back after us all. Do you think he won't kill Kahlan as well after he is finished with her?"

Richard frowned at her. "Are you saying we should run? That I should flee because of a witch's oath?" He gestured around at the room full of skinned corpses, some of them now sliced in half by the magic he used to stop the Glee. "That I should abandon the People's Palace to Michec knowing full well what a monster he is and what he will do?"

"No . . ." She shook her head in exasperation. "No. It's not that. It's just that with such grave danger to you and the Mother Confessor—and to your children—we don't have the luxury of that much time for a futile attempt to heal Vika. Nor can you afford the distraction of a protracted attempt that is doomed to fail in the end. The most you can do for Vika now is to grant her the mercy of a quick death. She has earned that much."

Richard bit back his anger at her words and instead said, "Let me handle this."

Seeing the look in his eyes, Shale finally relented with a nod. He gently pulled away from her grasp on his arm. Kahlan, then, touched him with an expression of anguish over the grim situation. Richard looked at both of them briefly, at the pain he saw in their eyes. The resolve they saw in his eyes kept them both from saying anything.

And then, something back in the darkness caught his eye. Past Kahlan and Shale, in the distance, in the dim greenish light, he saw a single Glee just standing there, watching. He remembered seeing a single Glee before, after a previous battle when he killed a large group of them.

He stared at the dark shape. It stared back.

And then it did the oddest thing. Without moving, it turned its hands over and spread the three claws of each hand and just stood there like that for a moment. He saw, then, that the Glee's hands were webbed between each claw.

It wasn't at all an aggressive posture. If he didn't know better, he would say it was acknowledgment of Richard and what he had just done. As soon as the Glee knew they had made eye contact, and it had shown him its webbed hands, the air turned to scribbles as it vanished back into its own world.

Richard wondered if it could possibly be the same one he had seen before, the same lone Glee. Or if it was a scout of some sort come to see what had happened and report back to the Golden Goddess.

He also wondered why the Glee would have webbed claws, if they were predators.

Whatever its purpose, Richard didn't have

time to consider it any longer. He had much more important things to tend to.

His gaze refocused on the two women in front of him. “I have to help Vika.”

5

The naked Mord-Sith lay in a pool of her own blood on the rough, cold stone floor below where she had been hanging. Bits of broken chain were scattered across the floor. Her single braid was soaked red from that blood. Her red leather outfit lay on the far side of her.

Vika's pale face was a landscape of bruises, open wounds, and strings of blood from a beating. Richard could see that both her cheekbones had been broken from blows. One of the bone fragments stuck out through the skin. He could hardly contain his rage at what the witch man had done to her. He could also hardly believe that she was still alive. He knew, though, that if he didn't do something soon, she wouldn't be alive for long.

He reminded himself that the time would come, but now was not the moment to focus on his anger at Moravaska Michec. Now, it was about Vika, and what he hoped to be able to do.

She was trembling ever so slightly. Her eyes were closed as she struggled against the crushing weight of pain. A glistening, bloody mass of her intestines lay up against her side, still attached by a knotted length of gut coming out of the gaping wound in her abdomen. He had a hard time believing that she wasn't crying in agony.

During their training, Mord-Sith were kept on the cusp of death for days on end. Richard knew that such twisted training made them more than merely tough. They all knew death well. They all danced with death in their own, private way. It was that training, he thought, and only that training, that made her able to endure it, and probably was keeping her alive.

Vika's eyes opened as Richard knelt down close beside her.

"You did good, Lord Rahl. I knew you would think of something if I could just buy you a little time." The inside of her lips had been gashed open on her teeth when Michec had struck her with his fists. He could see how much it hurt her to speak, despite doing her best not to let it show. "I hope you don't think I was really urging him to kill you."

"No," he quietly reassured her as he put a hand gently on her shoulder, "no, I knew what you were doing."

She let out a breath in relief.

Richard smiled down at her through the pain of empathy at seeing her in such a condition. He gently brushed a strand of blond hair back from her eyes as she gazed up at him.

"You are the one who did good, Vika. It was all your doing. I couldn't have done it without you. You saved Kahlan and me—and our children."

"It was my great honor," she said. "I'm afraid that it is my time, now. I know the cusp of the world of the dead well enough. I have returned from that place more times than anyone has a right to. I am looking out at you now from the brink of that dark place. The world of the dead calls to me. My time has come to go beyond the veil. Thank you for rescuing me from Hannis Arc and for allowing me to serve you."

Richard shook his head. "It's not your time,

Vika. Don't even think that. You must live. I need you."

She rolled her head from side to side. "It is too late for me now. I know that. Please don't try to soothe me with the false kindness of a lie. I know better."

"I am the Seeker of Truth. It is no lie. I wouldn't do that to you. If I thought it was too late for you, I would tell you so."

She smiled the littlest bit. "Not even you can heal me or hold back the world of the dead. But I would be eternally grateful if you would spare me any more suffering in this life and send me swiftly on to the next."

"Vika—"

"Please, Lord Rahl. End it. I am ashamed to admit that I am not strong enough to endure this any longer and I don't have the strength to end it myself. I hate for you to see me so weak. Please. Grant me the mercy of a quick death."

Richard swallowed back his anguish. It was hard for him to see her beg for death.

"I asked you to trust me. You must do that now. I am the Lord Rahl. We are bonded in an oath—you to me and me to you. Your life while in this world is in my hands and just as it is your duty to serve and protect me, my duty is to protect you. More than that, I need you. You have given me your oath of loyalty. Remember that oath now and put your trust in me. You must hold on for me."

Before she could object, Richard laid a hand gently on her brow. He closed his eyes and bowed his head, letting his power flow into her. Vika gasped as she felt the hot rush of it. He didn't try to heal her, or even relieve her pain. He knew that would be futile right then. For the moment, he could only give her strength to help her endure her injuries and hold on until he could do more to try to save her.

When he opened his eyes and lifted his head, he was looking into her intense blue eyes. He smiled at the look in those eyes.

"There is the Mord Sith I know." He touched a finger to her lips before she could speak. "My strength is your strength. Now, hold on for me."

A tear ran from the corner of her eye as she nodded.

Richard rushed to his feet. He might have given her some added strength, but he knew he didn't have much time. Strength alone would not keep her alive.

A short distance away, Shale, keeping a watchful eye on him, was just finishing helping Kahlan get her clothes back on. Kahlan's eye was still bluish black and swollen shut. Her wrists oozed blood, as did Shale's wrists, as did his own.

"Watch for Michec," he told them both. "He is still down here, somewhere. We are going to need some time without being interrupted."

Shale eyed him suspiciously. "Time for what?"

Kahlan was just finishing buttoning her shirt. When Richard didn't answer, she offered her own answer. "Time for a crazy idea, I suspect."

Shale looked to Richard and then back at Kahlan. "What crazy idea?"

"I can't begin to imagine."

"Kahlan, I need you to do something." With an arm around her shoulders, Richard pulled her closer. He didn't have time for questions. "I know you are hurting and you need to be healed. So do Shale's wrists. We will take care of that, I promise. But right now, stay here with Vika. I don't want her to be alone. Hold her hand. Just be with her until I get back."

"Where are you going?"

"To get the others."

Shale gestured off toward where the rest of

the Mord-Sith knelt at the opening to the kill room. "Michec blocked them. Do you believe it is the same kind of trick of magic that he did with us?"

Richard sighed as he looked off among the hanging corpses toward the opening to the room. In the distance, between some of the skinned bodies, he could just see the red leather outfits of a few of the kneeling Mord-Sith.

"No. He was a trainer of Mord-Sith. I don't know exactly how such things worked, but as a trainer he would possess very real power over them. I'm sure Michec really was able to block them off from everything."

"Then what are you going to do?" the sorceress asked.

"I'm going to pull them out from beyond that block. Now wait here with Kahlan, please, and stay on guard. Michec is out there, somewhere, and sooner or later he is going to come after us. I'm worried he might slip back in here and surprise us."

"When you see him are you going to scythe him down with light from your sword like you did to the Glee?" the sorceress asked expectantly. "That would certainly be effective."

Richard's mouth twisted with frustration. "I would if I could, but I don't actually know how I did it. I simply reacted. In that instant of desperation I can only assume my war-wizard heritage took over, assessed the nature of the threat, what tools I had at hand, and what powers could be brought to bear, then it did what that instinctual part of my ability concluded would be the most effective response. I don't know that for certain, but it seems the most logical guess. I do know it wasn't a conscious act."

Shale briefly considered his words. She finally gave him a serious look. "Then what are you going to do if you encounter the witch man? He has powerful magic."

Richard gazed back with an equally serious look. "I guess I'll have to take care of him the old-fashioned way."

"The old-fashioned way? What's that?"

Richard arched an eyebrow. "I'll just have to go all emotional on him."

Shale's mouth twisted with displeasure as she looked over at Kahlan. "You were right. A crazy idea."

6

Just before he reached the broad opening back out to the corridor, Richard paused, sword in hand, to carefully lean out and look in both directions. He could feel the word "TRUTH" formed by the gold and silver wire-wound hilt pressing into his palms. Blood ran down from the painful, throbbing wounds on his wrists, onto the hilt of the sword, and then down the blade to drip from the tip. His blood always made the sword's magic lust to meet the enemy. He had often used his blood to give the sword even more motivation.

Looking out, he didn't see any sign of the witch man. He worried how Michec might be able to hide himself in plain sight. After all, the first time Richard had seen him he had seemed to materialize out of smoke. Fortunately Richard didn't see any smoke, either. But he had no way of knowing what other powers Michec might be able to use to hide himself.

Richard had kicked the man in the head pretty hard, but he didn't know exactly where his boot had connected or how much damage it had done. All he knew was that he had used all his strength to do it. With the way it had knocked the man out cold, it had to have done some damage, but Richard didn't know if it was enough.

Michec was most likely hiding somewhere nursing his injuries. Richard knew nothing about witch men and wondered if it was possible for him to heal himself. Unless the kick had done serious damage, it wouldn't keep him down.

Someone that filled with hate and a lust for power wasn't about to let his prey slip away, so Richard knew it wouldn't be long before the witch man came out of nowhere to attack them. When he did, Richard knew, the man would be out for blood. But until then, he had at least a small window of opportunity to try to save Vika.

The other five Mord-Sith were still kneeling in a line in the broad opening, hands held out, their Agiel, still attached by the fine gold chains around their wrists, resting across their upturned palms. They all stared blankly ahead. Richard knew that despite their lifeless appearance, they would all feel the pain of those Agiel.

Richard didn't believe it had been a trick that put the Mord-Sith into such a state of oblivion. This was a result of Michec's abilities both as a witch man and as a trainer of Mord-Sith. Richard didn't know what those abilities entailed or how he had come by them, but he knew they were very real. It was just one more cause for concern. While young women were chosen for their innocence and compassion, he suspected that trainers of future Mord-Sith were chosen for their obsession with cruelty.

All he knew for sure was that he had to get the five Mord-Sith back from that lost place before he tried to heal Vika, and he needed to hurry; Vika couldn't last much longer.

He put his hand on the red leather on Berdine's shoulder. She didn't respond. She had belonged to Michec once, so his control over her would be the strongest. Through his hand on her shoulder Richard could feel the painful hum of power coursing through her from her

Agiel. That power was fueled by their bond to the Lord Rahl, not Michec, and therein lay the source of his hope.

He could also sense, through that connection, that she was in pain. That pain was likely worsened by the block. It saddened him, too, to feel her hopelessness.

Richard squatted down, keeping his hand in contact with her shoulder. He knew how to heal with his gift. He had, a number of times, connected to people who were injured or sick and let his ability flow into them. He began to open that same mental gateway deep within himself.

"I am here with you, Berdine," he said into her ear. "As Mord-Sith, your loyalty and bond are to me as the Lord Rahl for as long as you wish to serve me. No other may claim dominion or authority over you. No one. Not now, not ever. Moravaska Michec is an enemy of the D'Haran Empire and I am the leader of that empire. I now dissolve any block he placed in you and place instead the protection of my gift to block him from ever again using his power over you."

Richard removed the rest of his own internal restraints to let the full healing force of his power rush into her so she would not only hear him, but feel him, feel his gift, feel his bond to her and hers to him, and be able to feel the raw pain of the block the witch man had left in her mind melt away into nothingness.

He stood, then, and held the point of the sword over her upturned hands to let some of his blood drip from the tip of the blade onto her palms.

"With my bond and blood oath I reclaim you from that witch."

Berdine gasped. Her head jerked up. Her eyes came open. She blinked a moment and then shook her head as if gathering her senses, trying to understand where she was. Finally, she stared at the blood on her palms and then looked up at Richard.

"Lord Rahl . . ."

When Richard smiled, she suddenly shot to her feet and threw her arms around him in relief.

"You saved me! You came for me and you saved me! I knew you would."

Richard patted her back and then pushed away. "We don't have much time. I need to get the others back as well."

He went to each Mord-Sith in turn and repeated the procedure until all five of them were jolted out from behind that block Michec had put in their minds. None of the others hugged him the way Berdine had, but they were all clearly thankful that he had come for them and succeeded in breaking the witch man's hold over them.

"Where is Michec?" Rikka asked as she stood and looked both ways down the corridor.

"I don't know," Richard said. "We are going to need to hunt him down, but first I have to help Vika."

"You found her, then?" Nyda asked, expectantly.

Richard nodded. "I'm afraid that the news is not good, though. He hurt her bad."

Richard hurriedly led them back through the forest of nearly skinless corpses. The Mord-Sith all looked about dispassionately, taking in the exposed red muscles, white ligaments, and faces frozen in horror and agony. They were all familiar with Michec's work. When they spotted Vika, though, they were clearly angry.

"Michec did this to her?" Cassia asked in a whisper as she leaned in close.

Richard nodded. "We need to help her."

Nyda turned an incredulous look back over her shoulder at him. "Help her?" A look of sudden understanding came over her. She lowered her voice. "Oh, I see now what you mean. Lord Rahl . . . would you rather one of us do it, then? She is a sister of the Agiel, after all."

Richard cocked his head. "Do what?"

Nyda looked clearly uncomfortable. "You know. End it. A quick twist of my Agiel and her suffering will be forever over."

Richard held out his hands, forestalling any such idea. "No, no. You don't understand. We have to heal her."

7

The five Mord-Sith shared a look but didn't say anything. They all knew that these kinds of injuries were well beyond healing. Richard hoped to prove that belief wrong.

Kahlan was kneeling beside Vika, with Shale on the other side. Each was holding a hand of the gravely wounded Mord-Sith.

"We need to get on with the healing," Richard told them. He looked around to make sure all of them were paying attention. "We have to hurry. Here is what we are going to do."

Shale looked up at him. "We?"

Richard nodded as he gestured for all of the Mord-Sith to gather round closer to Vika so he would only have to explain it once.

"Michec is down here somewhere," he said,

looking to each of their faces in turn. "He could show up at any moment, so we can only do this if we're quick."

Shale clearly looked confused. "Healing grievous wounds, if it was still within the realm of possibility and if it could be done at all, would take a day at least, likely many days for all I know."

"You're right," Richard said. "We don't have that kind of time. Neither does Vika. So trying the conventional way of healing that you know so well is simply not an option. Not only that, but like you, I seriously doubt that it would even work. Whatever we do must be done quickly."

Kahlan looked puzzled as to what he could be talking about. Shale was looking at him as if he had lost his mind.

"Quickly," the sorceress repeated. "You intend to heal her quickly. Of course." She looked up at the ceiling as if speaking to an audience in a gallery. "That makes sense."

Ignoring Shale's remark, Richard wiped a hand across his mouth as he turned around, staring off in the other direction for a moment, trying to think how he could explain it to them without causing them to panic. He turned back.

"I think I have a way that we can heal her if we all do it together. All nine of us together."

"Lord Rahl," Berdine said as she gestured at her sisters of the Agiel to each side of her, "we don't know anything about healing. I think most of us have been healed at one time or another, but we can't heal anyone. We can't use magic—other than that which the Lord Rahl gives us through our bond in order to use the power of our Agiel and all that involves."

Richard knew quite well how much Mord-Sith hated anything to do with magic. "Yes you can," he insisted. "But in a unique way. I'm afraid that it will be dangerous, though. Dangerous to all of us. Still, I think it has a chance to be successful."

"You 'think'?" Shale held up a hand to stop him right there. "First of all, I can't imagine what you are talking about, but more importantly, you and the Mother Confessor have a responsibility to the two children of D'Hara she is carrying. Our job is to protect her from danger, not put her in it."

"This is to protect her," Richard insisted. "You need to listen to me. You all need to listen to me. You need to see the bigger picture, not just this one moment, this one risk. It's important that Vika live because she is vital to our survival. There are nine of us. If we lose Vika, then there are only eight."

Kahlan squinted. "Does this have something to do with the Law of Nines?"

Richard gave her a firm nod. "Yes."

"The law of what?" Shale asked. "I think you said something about that before."

"I did." Richard pointed a finger up at the palace above them. "In one of the highly restricted libraries up in the People's Palace, there is a book that deals with the power of numbers as it relates to the use of the gift. It says that there are various cardinal numbers, some of them very powerful in how they affect magic.

"Nine in many ways is the most important number. In the right circumstances it can alter and increase the power of magic. In some cases it can even invoke some powers of magic. In rare cases there are even powers of magic that can be brought about in no other way.

"The number three is associated as an element of the number nine, and so also important.

It's part of how we use magic. For example, the devotion is repeated three times. There's a reason for that. Those three repetitions reinforce the magic in the bond itself because they invoke the Law of Nines."

Berdine looked puzzled. "But three isn't nine."

"But there are three devotions spoken, three times a day. Three threes are nine. See what I mean? Three is a constituent component of nine. It adds power to an already powerful number."

"So you think that because there are nine of us, our power is greater than any one of us alone?" Kahlan asked.

"Among other things," Richard said, relieved that she, at least, grasped what he was talking about.

"What other things?" she asked.

Richard gestured overhead. "We are in the People's Palace, drawn in the shape of a spell-form to give the Lord Rahl more power. On top of that, we are also inside a complication, designed to make the Lord Rahl's power, aided by that spell-form, more effective. The Law of Nines makes a third element. All three of these things—the Law of Nines, the palace spell, and the complication—give me the best chance to save Vika.

"I have to take this opportunity while I have all those elements on my side."

Kahlan leveled a look at him. "We also have things that work against us. Besides Vika's wounds being grave, Michec is down here somewhere. He could show up and attack us at any moment. And then there are the Glee."

Richard nodded. "I didn't say it would be easy, or that there aren't risks." He leaned closer to her. "But if we lose Vika, we lose a powerful element of protection for you and the babies in getting us to the protection of the Wizard's Keep. To preserve that power of nine, we need Vika with us. We can't begin to imagine right now how and when we might desperately need that added bit of help afforded by the Law of Nines. As small as that bit of magic may be, it could be enough to make the difference when it matters most.

"Because of the Law of Nines, the nine of us together have a kind of cumulative ability that none of us alone would have. Neither Shale nor I by ourselves have the ability to do a healing of injuries as life-threatening as the ones Vika has."

Shale was giving him a look, part skepticism and part analytical interest. "So, because of this Law of Nines, you think all of us together can somehow heal her?"

"In a way, yes."

"In a way." Shale folded her arms. "How?"

"We need to all join hands. Shale, you will be holding Vika's right hand as you were a moment ago. Then all the Mord-Sith will line up around Vika, all holding hands. Kahlan will be at the end of them, then me. I will be holding Vika's left hand with my right, in that way linking us all together. When we are joined in that ring, I believe the Law of Nines will give me what I need to help me heal her."

Shale still had her arms folded as she glowered at him from under her brow. "And how long do you think this will take?" By her tone, she was clearly growing even more suspicious of exactly what it was he intended to do.

"From our side it will be almost instantaneous. That's the advantage of what I plan to do."

Kahlan leaned in, her suspicion now exceeding Shale's. "From our side? What exactly are you saying?"

Richard didn't want to fool any of them, but at the same time he had to tell them at least part of what he intended. "Once we are linked, I will use all our combined gifts to stay connected to Vika in the underworld."

Jaws dropped.

Kahlan reached out and gripped his arm. "What?"

"It's the only way."

Shale's arms had come unfolded as she leaned in along with Kahlan. "The only way to do what? Die with her?"

"Well, I should hope not," Richard said, offering a smile to her surprise. That clearly wasn't what any of them expected to hear. "You have to trust me on this. It's the only way to have the time we need to do this."

Only Kahlan understood. "Of course . . . but Richard—"

"Of course what?" Shale interrupted.

Kahlan cast a worried look at the sorceress. "The underworld is eternal. There is no such thing as time in an eternal world, because with no beginning and no end there is no way to measure it or determine how much time has passed. What might be an instant here could be days, or even centuries in the underworld."

Richard could see that Shale was about to unleash a hundred questions and a thousand objections. He didn't want to hear any of it.

"I intend to save Vika, the same as I would save any of you. I view this as necessary to help us get Kahlan and these children of D'Hara to the safety of the Keep. It needs to be done. We are wasting time."

In the underworld he would have an eternity of time, among other things.

"I want everyone to kneel down around Vika in a circle," he told them. "Shale, you take her right hand. The rest of you join hands like I explained. Kahlan, you take my hand."

"Lord Rahl," Vika said in a weak voice as they all knelt around her, "I don't want to endanger any of you. Please don't—"

"It endangers us more if we lose you. As the Lord Rahl I judge that this is what we must do. Now, put your trust in me." Richard gestured to the others. "Everyone, join hands."

8

Richard picked up Vika's Agiel, which he had pulled from her gut wound earlier and had thrown on the floor.

"Vika, I want you to hold this in your teeth. I gave you some of my strength, before. Do you think you can do that? I need you back at that place."

Knowing that he meant that place on the cusp between worlds, she nodded. In a way, the pain of an Agiel was an insane kind of familiar comfort to a Mord-Sith. Richard had already tensed the muscles of his abdomen to help him endure the pain of holding the Agiel. Unlike the Mord-Sith, he found no comfort in such pain. When he held it out in front of her she pulled her lips back and clamped her teeth down on it.

Her pupils dilated as the wall of pain hit her and her jaws clenched tighter.

He didn't need to tell her to bite down.

Once he saw that she had, he carefully picked up the small pile of her intestines coiled on the floor beside her. He did his best to carefully wipe off any specks of dirt or crumbled rock. Once he had inspected them to see that they didn't have any foreign matter stuck to them, he stretched out and pushed the tips of his fingers into the wound in order to spread open the sides to give him room to guide the warm mass back inside her abdomen.

Her eyes wide, Vika stared at the ceiling as she trembled. Each breath was a ragged pull; then she would tighten her muscles and bear down again until she needed another breath.

"All right, that's the worst of it," he told her.

She nodded without looking over at him. It didn't look like it had helped with the pain. Her face had gone a bloodless white, telling him that, if anything, the pain was worse.

He put a bloody hand on her shoulder. "Hold on, Vika. It won't be long. You are already on the cusp. The pain of the Agiel will help you take that final step through the veil. I will be holding your hand. I will be here, but also with you, and watching over you when you cross over."

The last part wasn't exactly true, but he needed to say it for those listening, especially Kahlan. This was no time for questions he dare not answer honestly.

"When you get to that place beyond, to that world, it will be tempting to let yourself go into that forever world," he told her. "Believe me, I know. You will find comfort there in being free of the pain, free of misery, fear, and worry—free of everything. You will want to let yourself drift away into that eternal world where struggles of life are a thing of the past and you can be at peace. If it's all too much for you, you have my permission to accept that world."

He didn't want her to make that choice, but he wanted to give her a choice to be better able to endure what she was about to face. He knew that by having the option of a way out, it sometimes helped endure a hard choice.

"But I need you, Vika. Kahlan needs you. Our children need you. D'Hara needs you. So I hope you will have the strength to let me heal you while your spirit is there and then return to us."

She finally looked over into his eyes and nodded. He could see her doing her best to fight the pain of both her injuries and the Agiel she held clamped in her teeth.

"This is insanity," Shale said in a low voice.

Kahlan looked like she might agree, but she didn't say so. Richard knew that despite her well-founded fear, Kahlan was doing her best to put her trust in his judgment that what he was doing was necessary to help get their unborn children to safety. He fervently hoped that her trust was warranted.

Richard looked up at the sorceress on the other side of Vika. "You may be right. I do know that without you to make up nine of us, this will likely fail. But just as I'm not forcing Vika to do this, I'm not forcing you to be a part of it, either. If you can't commit to helping me, to helping us all, and especially to helping Vika, then that must be your choice. Either way, I intend to attempt it, with or without you, but without you, without the Law of Nines as an aid, my chances of being successful go down. So it's up to you." He leaned a little closer to her across Vika's body. "Choose."

Shale's gaze took in all the Mord-Sith on their knees around the supine Vika. She met Kahlan's gaze for a long moment, but Kahlan, despite the bruises and the eye swollen nearly shut, was wearing her Confessor's face. Finally Shale looked down at Vika, the Agiel between her teeth as she did her best to draw each breath. At last, she looked back up at Richard.

"I didn't come all the way from the Northern Waste to deny you my help now. You are the Lord Rahl. Do as you must. I will support you."

Richard smiled his appreciation. "All right, I want everyone to concentrate on Vika. Imagine giving her your strength and imagine her being whole again. Shale, please add what ability you have at healing to mine."

"Do you really think that will help?" Cassia asked. "Us concentrating on Vika, I mean? We can't do magic."

"You're not doing magic. You are magic, through the power of the Law of Nines and through your bond to me. You are part of that whole. It's that whole that matters.

"You and your sisters have all been on the

cusp of death. You remember being partway into that world, don't you?"

Cassia looked grim. "More times that I care to remember."

"When you are on the cusp, you are actually partially in the underworld, or you couldn't really know that you were on the cusp, now could you? Vika knows. She is there now at that threshold, at the brink of death itself. She told me that she was already in some ways looking out at me from the world of the dead. It is that experience of being on the cusp that you bring to the circle. It is that experience of coming back into the light of this world that we need. Vika is crossing over as we speak.

"Now please, all of you, just do as I ask. I have to save her while I still can. We are all holding hands to give Vika a link back to this world. You know both. This is a time when we show how much life means to us all. You all are her sisters and her way back."

Vika squeezed his hand at his words. As she trembled from the pain of the Agiel clamped between her teeth, a tear rolled from the corner of her eye. Holding her hand, he could feel the pain pulling him under with her. He had to will himself to ignore it to do what needed to be done.

Richard squeezed Kahlan's hand. Her wrist was still oozing blood. He needed to heal that as well, to say nothing of the obviously painful, swollen bruises on her face.

Once they all had gone quiet, with their eyes closed and heads bowed, Richard turned his mind to what he needed to do, to what he couldn't tell them he was going to do. He took a deep breath against the enormity of the task ahead of him.

If he was to have the time necessary to do what needed to be done, the only place with enough time was a place without time.

He remembered all too well dying and going beyond the veil. He remembered all too well being in the world of the dead. As he concentrated, he embraced the devastating pain of the Agiel radiating up his arm to the base of his skull as motivation to help him go to that numb place of refuge from the pain of life. Thankfully, the others, because Vika's Agiel had never been used against them, could not feel the pain he felt from it.

With the overpowering need of being free of pain pushing him ever onward, he used the power of his gift to do one of the most frightening things imaginable.

He willed his heart to stop.

He ignored the crushing pain that started radiating from the center of his chest by concentrating instead on the pain of the Agiel that didn't let up even though his heart had gone still.

He felt Kahlan's hand tighten on his as she sucked back a sob of fear for him, not really realizing what he had just done.

The world faded away. Kahlan's grip seemed to dissolve as his muscles went slack. Richard saw darkness beyond darkness.

He heard the faint sound of voices—the countless voices of the dead from beyond the veil. As he sank into that dark void, swirling masses of souls swept through a darkness blacker than black and began to surround him. In that void, ghostly arms and writhing fingers reached for him. Hints of light wheeled around him. He held on to Vika, knowing that she was seeing the same thing.

Richard did his best to ignore the voices

and the reaching hands. He did his best not to recognize the spectral faces. He couldn't afford the distraction of familiar voices, familiar faces, familiar emotions and longing.

Despite his best efforts, those he had killed, evil people who fought in the world of life for the cause of death, smiled out at him from the darkness as they swept in closer, eager for the chance to rip and tear at his soul. Claws sank painfully into his spirit. As they tried to drag him down among them, Richard held onto an awareness of the light from above, of the light of Kahlan's soul and those with her beyond the veil. As he did, evil lost its grip on him and sank away. He pulled Vika up with him, away from the terrible evil that lusted for them both.

As they rose up through endless darkness, the multitude of souls appeared to be nothing more than the soft flickers of stars massing and moving together like folds of gossamer in a faint breeze, rippling, twisting, rolling as one insubstantial mass. Even as they revolved around him, a curtain of eternal inhabitants of darkness, they knew he did not belong.

But they wanted him to.

They whispered to him, promising him the end of pain, the end of sorrow, the end of a life of constant struggle. They whispered to Vika as well.

He had but to let himself accept what was all around him.

He knew that they were also appealing to Vika to join them in their eternal rest. He knew how much those whispers and tender touches would lure her toward their world for all eternity. He knew how she ached to accept their call.

Richard circled a comforting arm around her shoulders as she gazed about in wonder, the pain of the world of life far distant. In this dark world, she was free of the mortal pain of her injuries, even if her physical form was not yet free of those injuries. Richard held her close, silently reassuring her that he was with her, not letting her feel alone.

When she listened to him, the darkness shifted, the souls twisting away as if in eddies from a current sweeping past, carrying them with it. Richard held Vika close as the two of them drifted through layers of darkness teeming with spirits. Those streams of darkness carried them through rolling undercurrents formed out of nothing. All the time the soft glowing mass of souls followed along, distant, hesitant, yet drawn to them, these alien beings in their world. It was bewitchingly beautiful and terrifying all at the same time.

Richard had to remind himself continually of Kahlan's hand in his, still back there beyond the veil in the world of life, and his love for her. She and the other souls there with her were his anchor—and Vika's anchor—to the world back beyond the veil.

He had to remind himself of their two children back in the world of life. The twins needed him if they were to be born and their Graces were to be completed. And they all needed Vika. He wanted more than anything to be back with Kahlan, and with her unborn babies.

To do that, he needed to get on with the job at hand.

As Vika turned to him, not knowing what to do, not knowing what choice to make, he reached into himself to the depths of his gift, into the network of connections linking his magic to his soul, linking it to the world of life, searching for the exact gossamer threads he needed.

At the same time, he reached into Vika with his gift. Were they still in the world of life, she would have let out a gasp at the power of it.

9

Kahlan, her eyes closed, her head bowed, tried to focus her thoughts on Vika, hoping it would somehow help Richard heal her and at the same time keep her grounded in the world of life. Berdine, to Kahlan's left, held her hand in a tight grip that revealed her fears. Kahlan knew that, like her, they were all terrified by what Richard was doing. It involved magic that none of them understood and they all feared. Kahlan was only obliquely familiar with it, and her understanding of it was in large part theory. Sometimes, she had to put her trust in Richard even when she greatly feared what he was doing.

As the room grew deadly quiet, she couldn't seem to calm her anxiety.

In that silence, Kahlan heard a sound that didn't belong.

Oddly enough, it sounded like something wet.

With sudden realization of what it was, she opened her eyes, despite Richard's instructions, and glanced back over her shoulder. In the dim, greenish light beyond the forest of hanging corpses, she saw dark shapes running as yet more scribbles were forming in the air.

"Richard!" When he didn't respond, she screamed his name again.

Richard slumped, partly bent over on his side, one hand reaching back to hold hers, the other holding Vika's hand. Kahlan saw, then, that Vika had stopped breathing. She urgently pulled away from Berdine to put both hands on the side of Richard's chest, shoving him, trying to wake him from his state of deep concentration.

With a jolt of horror she realized that Richard wasn't breathing, either. She was momentarily confused, unable to understand why he would not be breathing.

If she lost him because she went along with his crazy idea, she would never forgive herself. The twins would never forgive her.

Despite her worry for him, there was no time to figure it out. She had to do something about the dire threat coming into their world from across the room. As she sprang to her feet, she stole a quick glance back to check that the sword was there at Richard's left hip. Once she saw it, she dropped down and grabbed the hilt. The blade rang, hot with rage, as she yanked it free of the scabbard. She knew that rage all too well.

"Shale!" Over on the other side of the still Vika, the woman's head was bowed, her eyes closed. "Shale!"

The sorceress's head jerked up. "What—"

More of the dark, wet shapes materialized out of nowhere to rush forward, their bodies steaming as they came around the hanging corpses. Clear, gelatinous blobs slid off them and splashed across the floor. She realized that was the wet sound she had heard at first.

"Do something!" Kahlan screamed at the sorceress in order to be heard over the sudden sound of murderous shrieks and howls from the Glee, excited at finding her vulnerable with no witch man to stop them.

One of the monsters, apparently the one she

had heard materialize first, was out well ahead of the others. She leaped back as wicked claws swiped at her, first one and then the other in rapid succession. Kahlan had been trained in the use of a sword growing up. She reacted instinctively. She swung the sword around and brought it down with all her might, lopping off the second arm that had taken a swipe at her, severing it between wrist and elbow.

The creature recoiled in surprise and pain, drawing back the stump. In that seemingly frozen instant, she immediately used the opening to drive the blade through its chest before it could use its other claw on her. The tall, dark shape dropped to its knees. The sword, still through its body and jutting out its back, was pulled down and almost out of her hands as the creature sank to the floor, already dead. Kahlan grunted with the effort of putting her boot against it and pulling the blade back out as the dark shape toppled over.

Dozens more Glee came charging out from among all the hanging bodies. Bloody sword in hand, Kahlan turned to the sorceress, now alert and on her feet.

"Do something! Richard's not breathing! He

can't help! I can't stop them all! You have to do something!"

Shale was already lifting her hands. With her eyes closed, her fingers twisted this way and that as she held her hands up before herself. When she opened her eyes, they had turned a strange yellowish color. Her long dark hair fell forward over her shoulders as her head and brow lowered, as if having no need to rush.

The dark material of the top she wore bunched above the leather forearm shields. Beads and small chains with strange amulets hung below a black leather bodice. A loose wrap skirt of dusky dappled colors was open at her left hip, revealing dark traveling trousers tucked into boots. The trousers had a variety of pockets and equipment straps.

Kahlan always thought of Shale as the sorceress who had healed her and saved the lives of her unborn children. She felt a bond to the woman because of that. But in that instant, her hands lifted up before her dark glower, her fingers swaying snakelike, Shale looked every inch a lethal witch woman. It was a frightening glimpse of pure menace.

As Kahlan swung back around toward the

advancing threat, sword at the ready, the floor suddenly came alive with snakes that seemed to materialize up out of the stone. The sight was as alarming as it was impossible.

She gasped as the writhing creatures slithered around her feet as they rushed toward the Glee. They brushed against her ankles as they went over her boots. Some of them glided in waves right over Richard's legs. There were so many the floor seemed to have suddenly come alive with movement.

Most were frighteningly big. While they weren't all the same color or type, most of the biggest were white. A few had brown patterns of scales. Some of the smaller black vipers had yellow bands with white and red rings. Others were a rust color, and a few of the smallest were no bigger around than her finger and as black as death. They were all shockingly fast.

Kahlan didn't know what kind of snakes were white, but these all had the broad heads and snouts of vipers. Red, forked tongues licked at the air as their bodies moved in writhing waves as they raced ahead. She saw that rather than round pupils, all of these snakes had slitted pupils.

Kahlan stood motionless, sword in hand, fearful that if she moved, the snakes still slithering around her ankles would turn and strike at her. As much as she hated and feared snakes, these didn't seem the least bit interested in her. From all around, the hundreds of vipers were all headed toward the Glee.

Shale hadn't moved. She stood with her hands lifted, her fingers slowly twisting with the effort of doing something that appeared extremely difficult. The witch woman's eyes had turned a darker yellow, and Kahlan could have sworn that they, too, had vertical slits for pupils, but before she could get a good look in the dim light, she had to turn back to the howling threat charging in toward them.

As a tall dark shape in the lead dove toward her, Kahlan brought the sword around in a mighty arc, lopping off its head. She had to turn and pull her hips sideways to avoid being knocked down as the headless monster toppled past her. The head bounced along atop the mass of snakes. In reaction to it landing on them, the snakes, with lightning quickness, turned and struck at the head with their fangs, so that as it tumbled along the floor, it became balled up in snakes.

Shale stood with her hands lifted, motionless other than her writhing fingers. Kahlan stole a quick glance and saw that all the Mord-Sith looked to be unconscious. Vika looked to be dead, as if she could no longer will herself to fight for life.

But far worse, that quick glance told her that Richard had clearly stopped breathing. At first, she had thought maybe he was holding his breath in concentration, but he would surely have responded to her calls, if not the threat from the Glee, if he could.

The mass of tall, slimy creatures slowed their advance, seeming unsettled by all the snakes racing toward them across the floor. First a few and then all the Glee came to an uneasy halt. They didn't look like they necessarily feared snakes, but the numbers and their behavior clearly had them concerned.

As they came to a halt, the racing snakes in the lead were finally close enough to strike. They lifted up and drew their heads back, the rest of their bodies whipping around forward for support, and then, jaws opened wide, they struck with lightning speed. As yet more came in, they threw themselves at the Glee. Fangs sank into the soft, dark flesh. The vipers struck at ankles, at legs, and the larger ones that could strike higher went for arms and the lean, muscular bodies.

When the vipers sank their fangs into the Glee, they didn't let go to strike again. Instead, they held on, their heads flexing as they pumped venom into their victims. The Glee, at first confused, then alarmed, were now in full fright, as each of them had dozens of vipers on them with more striking all the time. In mere moments, they were all covered with wriggling snakes. Arms weighed down by snakes that had sunk fangs into them became too heavy to lift. As they staggered back, the snakes wouldn't let go. The stricken Glee dragged the weight of snakes with them as yet more leaped up to join in the mass attack.

Other long, massively thick snakes, with mottled patterns of brown, black, and tan, coiled themselves around legs, progressively rolling the coils up the legs of the victim, finally wrapping their fat bodies around the chest and neck. Once they had made it up the dark, slimy body, they began rhythmically constricting. With each breath the victim took, the snakes tightened their bodies. Kahlan could see the panic in the big glossy eyes of a Glee, the third eyelid blinking in as it struggled to breathe. Each time the Glee breathed out, the snake tightened, preventing the Glee from getting a full breath. In this way, the powerful snakes worked to progressively suffocate the victim.

Some of the Glee, with snakes already attached to them as yet more vipers leaped at them to strike, began to vanish, retreating back into their own world. The snakes that missed an intended target that was suddenly no longer there dropped to the floor and without pause turned their attack to others still there. As many of the Glee vanished back into their own world, they took the snakes, with fangs firmly sunken into them, back with them.

Others had become so fearful of the attacking vipers that they didn't seem to have the presence of mind to flee. They fell back under the weight of snakes attached to them. Once on the floor, they were even easier prey. The Glee shrieked in pain and terror, swiping at vipers going for their faces. None of the invading Glee escaped the attack. Everywhere, snakes continued to attack, sinking their fangs into any victim they could get to.

As the last of the Glee still able were vanishing, Kahlan turned and fell on Richard. She pounded her fists against his chest.

"Richard! Richard! Come back! You have to come back!"

He didn't respond. He seemed lifeless. Kahlan had thought he meant that he was going to go to the cusp of the world of the dead with Vika. Clearly, he hadn't. He must have made some kind of miscalculation and crossed over into the world of the dead.

Or else he had done it deliberately.

And now he was trapped there.

"Shale, help him!"

Kahlan saw Shale, instead of responding to Kahlan's urgent call, sinking to the floor. The witch woman looked to be blacking out from exhaustion. The effort of conjuring all those snakes to attack the Glee seemed to have taken everything she had.

"Well, well, snakes, is it?" a gruff voice behind Kahlan said. "Witch women do seem to have a fondness for their snakes."

Kahlan spun to the terrible voice she knew all too well.

Michec extended an arm down toward the

writhing mass of snakes. One of the larger white vipers coiled itself around his arm, slithering up and around to settle itself over his shoulders. He stroked its head affectionately. The snake flicked its tongue and seemed to be content with its new master.

Michec casually swished a hand, and the hundreds of snakes massing around his feet began dissolving. He lowered the one draped over his shoulders to the floor, where it glided away until it, too, vanished.

10

Kahlan gripped the hilt of the sword tighter in both hands even though she remembered full well that it had somehow done Richard no good. If he hadn't been able to use the sword effectively against the witch man, she didn't know how she would be able to do any better. Still, it did make her feel better to have a weapon in her hands. She could feel the word "TRUTH" on the hilt made out of the gold wire wound through silver wire pressing against her palm. It was a reminder of all she and Richard had gone through since they met in the Hartland woods, all because of Darken Rahl, and now, all this time later, she faced one of his henchmen. It felt almost as if Darken Rahl himself was reaching out from the grave to continue to haunt them.

And like Darken Rahl, the witch man had some kind of powers that had counteracted the power in the sword and enabled him to capture Richard. She remembered Zedd telling him that the sword wouldn't work against Darken Rahl. She could only imagine that the same protection against the Sword of Truth might extend to Michec.

Still, it was all she had, unless she could unleash her Confessor's power on him. Not only was he keeping his distance, but it also seemed risky to attempt such a thing on someone with abilities she had never encountered before. She knew that there were rare people on whom her power had no effect, or an unpredictable effect. It could be that Michec was like that. If she had to, though, she fully intended to attempt it.

She started circling to Michec's left to draw his attention away from Richard, Shale, and the Mord-Sith, who were all on the floor and unresponsive. It seemed that when Shale used her ability to the extent she had against the Glee, it sapped her strength until she could recover. That was something Kahlan understood all too well. When she used her power, it took her time to recover. She didn't know what the problem was with Richard, and that worried her greatly.

For all practical purposes, she was the only protection for the others, and she was alone with this madman. By the look on his face, he clearly relished the idea of catching her by herself. As she slowly moved to the side, she watched for any opening in case she had to try to use her power on him.

She worried, too, that Michec might have had something to do with the condition of the others. The memory of being helpless with him about to skin her alive was all too fresh in her mind. Right then she felt very alone and vulnerable.

"Again with the sword?" Michec, seeming amused, arched an eyebrow over one eye. "You think yourself better with it than your husband? Well, should we see?"

He stomped a foot in her direction, bluffing that he was going to charge at her. Kahlan didn't flinch back. Instead she thrust the sword out at him, hoping to catch him off guard. She didn't know if the magic of the sword would work against him, but the razor-sharp blade was in itself formidable. He easily stepped back out of range of both her and the sword. Her caution kept her from following through and pressing the attack.

He grinned with menace. "Ah, a fighter. Good for you. I enjoy skinning fighters." He gestured at all the corpses behind him. "Makes it so much more satisfying when they finally find themselves helpless. I like to look into their eyes when I begin and they know that there will be no stopping and no rescue."

Kahlan didn't need to imagine such terror; she had been there. She wanted nothing more than to kill this monster.

She kept the point of the blade up and at the ready. She could feel its power singing through every nerve fiber in her body. The sword wanted the man's blood, but not as much as Kahlan did. She resolved that when he eventually came at her, she would try to run him through or use her power. What really concerned her was that he knew she was a Confessor but that didn't seem to bother him in the least. If both the sword and her power failed to stop him, well then, at least she would not go down without a fight.

She noticed, then, as she forced herself to look into his cruel eyes, that his face didn't look the same as she remembered. The shape was different. His features had always looked thick and blocky, but the area around his left jaw and ear appeared even thicker. She could see traces of blood left in the folds of his ear. It looked like he had wiped off blood that had been all over the side of his face.

She also saw that the filthy white robes he was wearing were stained with fresher blood up at the neck, as if it had run down onto his robes. That blood was not from a victim. It was his.

The injury had to have been from when Richard kicked the witch man in the head. She wondered just how much damage Richard had done. A kick that hard to his head, if in the right spot and if Richard had been able to make solid contact, would likely have broken the mandible. That would certainly explain why his speech sounded a little slurred, and also why he had been gone for a while. He had probably been hiding somewhere while he did what he could to repair the damage enough with his magic to keep going. As much as he tried not to show it, she could see by the way he kept his shoulder protectively forward that it was hurting him. She realized that might give her an opportunity.

But then, on the other hand, a wounded animal was more dangerous, and Michec certainly was an animal.

Together, with Michec glaring at her and Kahlan with the sword up at the ready and glaring back, they continued slowly revolving as if locked together. Michec seemed entertained by the dance as he waited for her to make the first move, or to make a mistake so he could overwhelm her.

Of course, it was also possible that he simply enjoyed the game.

As they slowly moved in unison, his dark eyes peering out from narrowed eyelids were about as intimidating as any she had ever seen. But she also thought she saw caution there. She hoped that Richard had managed to hurt the man more than she knew.

She also felt the weight of responsibility. It wasn't just her life she was protecting; it was the twins' and everyone else's. If she tried something and it turned out to be the wrong move, they would all be dead.

For the moment, as she and Michec both stared each other down, each waiting for the right moment to strike, she decided that if she saw the right opening, she would have to act.

His gaze, then, flicked down to something that caught his attention. His intimidating glare took on a hint of confusion.

Kahlan glanced down, looking for what it was that had him so distracted. She didn't see anything out of the ordinary.

"See something you don't like?" she asked. "Thinking twice about how this blade can cut you?"

He cocked his head as he appraised her with one eye. "I see you have managed to have your wounds healed while I was . . . away for a time." He arched an eyebrow. "I will soon remedy your return to good health and have you screaming your lungs out down here where no one other than your husband can hear you and no one will ever help you."

Her wounds? She didn't know what he was talking about.

She glanced down again, and then she saw it.

In the heat of the confrontation, she hadn't realized that her wrists were no longer cut up and bleeding from the manacles. They were completely healed and looked as if they had never been severely gashed. She reached up just long enough to feel that the left side of her face wasn't bruised and swollen, nor was it throbbing in pain. The cut along the side of her neck was gone as well.

He gestured behind at all the skinless corpses without taking his eyes off her. "As you can see, I have quite a talent. The time has come for me to demonstrate."

11

Just then Kahlan caught movement out of the corner of her eye. It was Vika, naked, with her Agiel between her teeth and a knife in her fist, charging in at a dead run. She was a picture of muscled fury.

At the last instant she rammed the knife into Michec's side, catching him off guard. Kahlan had thought that she would use the Agiel between her teeth, but she must have been more interested in cutting him open the way he had cut her.

He let out a terrible cry of pain and surprise as he fell away from her attack to escape her blade.

Michec twisted and spun to get some distance as she tried to cut him again, but missed. He clamped a hand over the wound. Kahlan could see the wet red stain under his hand growing on his filthy white robes.

He saw, then, the same thing Kahlan saw. As hard as it was to believe, Vika was completely healed. She didn't have on a stitch of clothes and they could clearly see that she looked in perfect health. The flesh of her abdomen was flawless and looked never to have had so much as a scratch. Kahlan couldn't imagine how her intestines could have been put back as well as they had and how such a gaping wound had completely closed.

In her hunger to cut Michec, Vika must have just had time to grab her knife from the sheath attached to her leather outfit. She screamed in fury as she scrambled to dive at him again and drive her blade into him again, but her bare feet slipped on the slime and blood all over the floor from the Glee. She leaped back up to her feet almost immediately.

The witch man moved faster than Kahlan would have thought his bulk would allow, spinning around twice so that Vika, on slippery footing in her bare feet, missed him when she took a swing and tried to slash him again. Though he escaped her stabbing him a second time, the first cut had obviously done damage.

Because of his girth, Kahlan suspected that the blade had cut only fat and muscle. She didn't think it had gone deep enough to damage internal organs. Vika had apparently been going for his kidney. Had she hit it, that would have stopped him or at least slowed him down enough for her to be able to finish him. As it was, he was still on his feet and while hurt, it was not enough to stop him.

Seeing an opportunity with Michec wounded, Kahlan cried out in fury of her own to startle him as she charged in at him sword-first. Even if the magic didn't work against him, the sharp blade would. Ordinarily, Kahlan would have been unsure that it would be so simple that she could kill him with Richard's sword, but the way Vika had driven her knife into him had clearly hurt the man. From behind Vika came flashes of red leather as the rest of the Mord-Sith raced to Vika and Kahlan's aid.

Hurt from Vika's first strike with her blade, Michec held one hand back to comfort the wound as he desperately swept his other hand up as if lifting a curtain before himself.

As his hand came up, the glass light spheres abruptly dimmed.

And then, the quickly waning light revealed nightmarish creatures densely packed together coming at them out of nowhere, all of them reaching with fury and lust.

They were terrors from a child's nightmares, larger than a person, most with veined, membrane wings like bats. Those wings stretched and flapped. At the first joint of the leading edge of their wings they had a large, hooked claw that raked the air as they swept their partially folded wings forward, trying to snag Kahlan or one of the Mord-Sith.

The pale, wrinkled, ulcerated flesh of the monsters was hairless. In places that flesh looked rotted away, exposing gooey green slime and fibrous tissue beneath, like the damp, rotting, decomposing tissue of a corpse. They glided in just above the floor, their wings flapping to enfold their prey. As they got closer, they opened huge mouths full of fangs.

Their jaws opened wide as they roared, so wide that it distorted and stretched the skin of their faces. That flesh tore in places, exposing the decomposing sinew beneath. Under the tears in the stretched flesh she could see their jaw and cheek bones. Flesh hung in ragged flaps as it ripped apart when their mouths stretched even wider to snap at Kahlan and the others frantically backing away.

Kahlan and all the Mord-Sith continued to scramble back, trying to avoid being caught by the grotesque creatures as they hurtled in out of the rapidly gathering darkness. Their deafening howls echoed through the room. In the fading light, Kahlan saw that the creatures were not all the same. Not all were winged like bats.

Some of the things had no wings, but instead had long, skeletal arms. They grasped at the air with bony fingers as they rushed in, reaching for Kahlan and the others. Some were missing part of their skull, exposing the festering brain and internal structures. Some of the forms had only scraps of skin attached to bones. That kind, their joints separating from the effort, ripped themselves apart as they struggled to leap through the air to be the first at Kahlan and the Mord-Sith.

Others, with long gangly limbs, crabbed sideways across the floor, ducking in under the winged creatures. Others staggered with stiff limbs and a halting gait. Most of their mouths opened impossibly wide, as if they intended to devour Kahlan and the others whole in one bite.

It was a collection of creatures beyond imagining. None of them could possibly be anything that existed in the world of life.

And yet, Kahlan realized that she had seen these things before.

A whole army of the monsters charged in at her, wings made of stretched skin flapping, raptorlike claws extended, lips pulling back in snarls over fangs. As Mord-Sith leaped toward her to help, Kahlan swung the sword, ripping through the monsters. The sword seemed to tear them apart rather than cut them. Their bodies disintegrated as if made of crumbly dirt and dust. Flesh and bone fell to pieces as she swung the blade as fast as she could.

It was growing so dark so rapidly that she already couldn't see the women fighting near her. But she could see the glowing red eyes of ever more of the things coming for her. She swung the sword as fast and hard as she could, knowing that if she stopped, they would be all over her. No matter how many she destroyed, their numbers pressing in at her seemed to multiply.

Only brief, terrifying moments after the battle had started, the room was plunged into total darkness. The blackness was filled with the terrible angry howls and ravenous screeches of the things coming at her and the others. Kahlan used their cries to find them, swinging the sword around when she heard them trying to get behind her. She had no hope but to keep fighting.

The darkness was so complete that the red glow of their eyes went dark, too, so that she could no longer even tell where the swirling mass of creatures were. In desperation Kahlan kept swinging the sword, hoping none of the Mord-Sith were close enough to get hit by the blade. She could feel the resistance each time it crashed through the monstrous things. She felt bony bits and reeking, wet scraps smacking into her as they disintegrated.

And then, when she knew that all hope was lost, the air suddenly seemed to explode. Flames filled the room, twisting, spiraling, rolling as if inside the inferno of a blast furnace. It was so bright Kahlan had to close her eyes and cover her face with a forearm against the blinding light and intense heat as she turned away. She feared she would be consumed in the conflagration.

Instead, the billowing flames were gone almost

as soon as they had erupted, so fast that they didn't burn her as she had thought they surely would; they didn't so much as singe her hair.

As the flames vanished and the room was once again plunged into blackness, the air was filled with a swirl of burning embers that slowed and finally drifted down, sparking out as they touched the stone floor. In the faint light of those glowing embers, Kahlan saw the Mord-Sith nearby, like her with their weapons held up defensively.

After a moment of total darkness and dead silence once all the burning embers were gone, the light spheres around the edge of the room slowly began to brighten again. In the faint greenish glow, she could see that all the corpses were still hanging throughout the room. She had thought they might have been ripped to shreds by the ravenous creatures or burned to cinders in the flames, but they looked untouched. Apparently, the beasts had only come for the living and the flash of fire was too brief to consume the bodies.

But the fire had incinerated the creatures, burning them to ash. It left behind the stench of sulfur.

"What were those things?" Vale asked in a panting whisper.

Kahlan knew what they were but was afraid to say it out loud.

"Where did he go?" Rikka asked in a heated voice as she and the others raced around, searching among the forest of bodies for the witch man.

Cassia dropped to the floor to look under all the hanging corpses to see if Michee was hiding behind one of them, perhaps in the distance. She finally jumped back up.

"I don't see him anywhere."

Shale raced up, coming in protectively close to Kahlan.

"What in the world were those things?" Nyda asked as she worked to catch her breath. "I've had nightmares that haven't been as scary as that."

Shale cast a sidelong look at Kahlan. "I can only conjure snakes. Apparently, the witch man has the power to conjure demons."

"Demons! Like from the underworld?" Nyda shook her head. "That can't be true."

"I've seen such things before," Kahlan said.

Nyda looked incredulous. "Where?"

"In the world of the dead," Kahlan finally told them in a troubled voice.

"You can't be serious," Shale said.

They all looked at Kahlan expectantly, awaiting more of an explanation.

"They're called soul eaters."

"Soul eaters!" Berdine exclaimed. "How could Michec bring demons from the underworld into the world of life?" She swept an arm out. "And what happened to them at the end? It was like they were suddenly exploded and burned to cinders."

"I have no idea," Kahlan said. "But from the smell of sulfur it seems clear to me that Michec somehow opened the veil enough to pull those things into this world to do his bidding."

"It doesn't matter, now. They're gone." Vika grabbed Kahlan's arm. "We have to help Lord Rahl. He healed all of us. We have to help him."

When a last, quick check around the room confirmed that Michec was nowhere to be seen and they knew that he wasn't about to set upon them again, Kahlan rushed over to Richard, dropping to her knees to see if he had started breathing yet. She was alarmed when she found that not only wasn't he breathing, he had no pulse.

"Richard!" She pounded his chest with her fist. "Richard!"

Shale leaned in close. She put a hand on his forehead, closed her eyes, and was silent for a moment.

The sorceress at last drew her hand back as if the touch had burned her fingers. She looked up at Kahlan, her eyes reflecting her horror. "He's . . . gone."

The Mord-Sith stared at her in stunned silence.

"He's not gone," Kahlan insisted. "He just needs our help to find his way back."

Shale's eyebrows lifted in disbelief. "From the dead? How do we help him do that?"

"He's not dead." Kahlan swallowed back her rising sense of panic as a vision of her children never knowing their father flashed through her mind. "He's just lost."

Shale gave the Mord-Sith watching her a troubled look before she looked back at Kahlan. "And how do you propose that we get him . . . unlost?"

12

Kahlan pressed her fingertips to her forehead as she frantically ran through memories and what she knew of the underworld, trying to come up with a way to get Richard back from that dark place. She stubbornly refused to believe the finality of it. She couldn't let herself believe the finality of it. But while she believed it might be possible to get him back, she also knew that the window to do so—even if it still existed—was rapidly closing.

At last, her head came up. She looked to all the faces watching her.

"The Law of Nines. Richard said that the Law of Nines is a trigger for magic."

Shale threw her hands up. "How is that supposed to help us? He is with the good spirits, now. He is beyond what we can do with magic."

"But for a precious bit of time, he still has a link here, in this world." Kahlan gestured. "Everyone gather around. Shale, you go on the other side of him and take his hand. I'll take this one." She urgently motioned the Mord-Sith to all come in closer. "The rest of you, kneel down around him and hold hands between Shale and me. We need to link us all together with Richard between me and Shale."

While they clearly didn't understand what it was that Kahlan thought they could do, they all gathered around Richard anyway, taking up each other's hands even though they all looked confused as to why they were doing it, hoping that somehow she knew some secret solution and could do what none of them could imagine.

"We all need to bow our heads and close our eyes," Kahlan told them.

Vale leaned in expectantly. "And then what?"

"And then . . . think about Richard. Think about how much we all want him back. How much we all need him back."

The Mord-Sith shared skeptical looks.

Kahlan thought of something else. She

released his hand and picked up the Sword of Truth. She placed the hilt in his hand, then put her hand over the other side and intertwined her fingers with Richard's, locking their hands together around the hilt of the sword. The word "TRUTH" on her side pressed into her palm. She knew that the same word on the other side was pressing into Richard's palm. That physical sensation was intimately familiar to both of them. More than that, the Sword of Truth was an ancient weapon with unfathomable magic. She hoped that magic would also help guide Richard back to them.

Tears ran down Vika's cheeks as she watched Kahlan position the sword. "If we don't get him back, I will never forgive myself. He did this for me. He came after me. I told him not to, but he did it anyway. He shouldn't have. I wish Michec had killed me, then Lord Rahl would not have done what he did and he would be here, alive, and with you all. He would be where he belongs."

"No, he wouldn't," Kahlan said, knowing how distraught the Mord-Sith would have to be to show such emotion. "None of us would be here. We would all be dead."

Vika wiped a tear back from her cheek. "What are you talking about?"

"When Richard found out that Michec had taken you and that he was here at the People's Palace, he wanted to get you back, but more than that, he knew as the Lord Rahl that we couldn't leave the witch man here when we leave for the Keep. You, of all people, know what Michec is capable of. He was devoted to Darken Rahl and hated that Richard was now the Lord Rahl. His ambition has no bounds. There is no telling what he might have done, but we do know that he would have worked to defeat all we have fought for. He has the power to undo all the good we have worked to bring about.

"We had to go after that monster. Yes, Richard wanted to rescue you, but he would have gone after Michec even if you were already dead. He had to. We came down here, into Michec's lair, and he was somehow able to capture us. That's not your fault. Richard was going after Michec one way or another, with you or without you."

"Yes but if I had already been dead—"

"Then you couldn't have saved us." Kahlan was shaking her head. "Don't you see? All the rest of us would have been captured whether or not you were alive. But since you were still alive, you were able to interrupt Michec when he was about to start skinning me alive. That gave Richard time to stop him. You saved our lives, Vika."

"Kahlan's right," Shale said. "I think it was that Law of Nines thing he told us about. It caused a change in the outcome. The nine of us together had an effect on what would otherwise have happened."

Kahlan leaned in a little toward the distraught Mord-Sith. "That's why Richard came after you: because we need you. Your life is important to all of us. We all need each other. There is power in the nine of us together. I thought he was only going to the cusp of the underworld to help you somehow, but for whatever reason, he crossed over."

"He came after me," Vika said, fighting to hold back her tears. "That's why he crossed over. He did it to heal me."

Kahlan gave her a hurried nod. "He saved you for a reason. Now, we need to save him."

"How?" Shale pressed, frantic for some kind of reason to believe it could really work. "He crossed over through the veil. We all know what that means. Dead is dead. How in the world do you propose to bring him back from the dead?"

"Dead is not always as dead as you might think." Kahlan gritted her teeth against the fear of giving in to the finality of such thinking. "Richard is not dead. Not yet. Not with finality. He has done this before. He's just lost. There is no sense of direction or scale in the underworld. It's eternal in every direction. He will be trying to come back to us now that he is finished with what he needed to do there, but he needs the light of our souls to find his way back."

"But how can we reveal our souls to him when he's on the other side of the veil?" Shale asked.

"Like I said before, Richard told us that the Law of Nines is a trigger for magic of great power."

Shale looked far from satisfied. "But how—"

"Enough! We're wasting what precious little time we have! Bow your heads," Kahlan ordered, her patience at an end, "and give him a way back before he is gone too long and can't ever return."

A worried Berdine glanced over at Richard.

"Are you sure he hasn't already been gone too long?"

"Do it!" Kahlan yelled, her frantic fear powering her voice. "Do it now. Think of Richard and how much he means to each one of you and how much we all need him back. We need to show him the light of our lives on this side to guide him back through the veil. He is the completing link for the Law of Nines, the last one that makes nine of us. He is the Lord Rahl. Our bond to him as the Lord Rahl is our connection to him. Now use it.

"Rikka, Nyda, Cassia, Vale, Berdine, Vika, you have all been to the cusp before. Do that now if you can so that you can bring us all closer to that world."

When Kahlan was sure that all of the rest of them were following her orders, she finally bowed her own head.

She refused to allow herself to fear it wouldn't work. Richard would see the light of their souls on their side of the veil and it would help guide him back. She knew it would.

Just before she let herself slip into the memory of what it was like in that other place, she had a last twinge of fear that Michec might show up and, seeing them all vulnerable, slaughter every last one of them right then and there where they were kneeling.

Among the corpses, the room was dead quiet as she brought up a memory of the world of the dead, and her love for Richard, the father of her two children. Three, she corrected herself. One was gone now, but the twins were still growing in her.

She remembered, then, the first time she knelt before him and swore on her life to protect him. She had been the first ever to swear loyalty to him.

Her breathing along with everyone else's slowed almost to a stop.

13

Kahlan seemed lost in a quiet, lonely place on the fringes of panic when she heard Richard gasp in a breath.

She looked up into the life in his gray eyes, startled at him returning so abruptly. He smiled at her, too busy getting his breath to speak right then. Her fears, which she had been keeping under tight rein, were unexpectedly dispelled. Joy rushed in to displace despair.

Kahlan needed something more than words, though. She fell on him where he sat, holding him tight, feeling the life in him as his big arm came around to embrace her and pull her tight against him. It was salvation, redeeming her as she had been about to give up all hope.

"Lord Rahl!" Berdine squealed. "You're back! You're really back!"

He nodded, still panting.

Shale looked astonished. "How are you here? How is this possible?" The way she said it made it sound as if his return was almost unjust, a violation of everything she believed.

Richard swallowed, still catching his breath. He looked around at the forest of dead bodies, the empty vessels for souls now gone, perhaps, Kahlan thought, seeing them in a new and sympathetic light.

"I was lost. It's beyond dark, there." His haunted tone reflected everything behind those words. "I didn't know where the veil was, or how to find my way back. Then I saw the cluster of light of your souls, the glimmer of your lives gathered together around me to show me the way back. That was what I needed."

Berdine shook a finger at Kahlan. "That's just what she said would bring you back!"

Richard chuckled. "I'm glad you listened to her. You all brought me back. Thank you."

"The Law of Nines was the key," Kahlan said.

Richard nodded, still drawing deep breaths. "It was the trigger for magic that made it work."

Shale leaned in, looking bewildered to see him alive after being so clearly dead. She held up her wrists before him.

"We're healed." It sounded like an indictment. "Not just Vika. Kahlan and my wrists, and her face—we are all healed."

Richard nodded. "I know. I healed Vika, then I healed the rest of us as well." He ran a finger down Kahlan's once bruised and swollen cheek and then held up his own wrists to show them that they, too, were no longer cut and bleeding.

Shale seemed to be bursting with questions. She started one, only to stop and start a different one. Finally she was able to settle on one and get it out.

"Lord Rahl, how could you have healed Vika? Her wounds were well beyond healing, but even if they hadn't been quite so horrific and had been within the realm of the possible for healing, it would have taken many days to do such a complex healing. How is it possible that you healed her of such grievous wounds in the blink of an eye?"

Richard gazed into her eyes, looking for a long time as if gazing into her soul. "It was far more than the blink of an eye. The underworld is eternal. It never ends, so there is no such thing as time there. I could have taken months to heal her for all I know—there is no way to tell. In fact, it felt in many ways that I was there for that long. But here, despite how long I was there, only moments had passed. That was how my body survived until my soul could return. I was still connected to it through the Grace. There, those moments are an eternity that gave me the time to do what I needed to do. In a way, I was working in both worlds at the same time."

The answer appeared to be worse than no answer to the sorceress. "Working in both worlds?" Shale pressed a hand to her forehead, looking exasperated as she tried to imagine the unimaginable. She pressed her palms against the side of her head, elbows up, looking like she feared she was descending into madness. "How is that even remotely possible?"

Richard shook his head as he sighed. "The only way I can begin to explain it is that there, in the underworld, I'm able to see and touch the threads of my gift in ways that I never could here, in this world. You might say that the lines of the Grace are revealed to me when I'm there.

"Those tendrils are more pure, more amazing, than any of us realize of ourselves. Things I could never do here, things I couldn't even imagine doing, I can do there by touching the right strands in that line from Creation. It is beyond wondrous."

He gestured toward Kahlan's belly. "Those two lives growing in Kahlan are in the process of connecting all the countless filaments and fibers that will make up the lines of the Grace within each of them. We draw a representation of the Grace, but it is so much more than those simple diagrams. Each line is complex beyond our ability to comprehend.

"When I was beyond that outer circle of the Grace that represents the beginning of the underworld, I was able to see and touch those fibers, those strands and filaments, that connect us all to Creation. It's more than merely life, Shale. It is all of Creation, the totality of it all. It is life and the absence of life, all connected within the Grace which we each have within ourselves."

Shale bowed her head as she closed her eyes, fingers against her forehead. It looked like it was beyond overwhelming for her to fit it all into her understanding of the nature of the world of life. Kahlan reached over and put a hand over the sorceress's other hand in her lap, giving her confusion and disbelief a bit of silent empathy.

"Believe me, I, too, have trouble comprehending it all."

Even though Kahlan had been in that place, and understood some of what Richard said, he had been born a wizard, and he had a much deeper understanding of all those things. It was hard for her to remember the time when she had first met him, and he knew nothing about magic, and she had to teach him some of what she knew about it. He had come a long way. His understanding of it all had at some point surpassed hers. In some ways, it was hard to even grasp the reach of his awareness.

Vika was already up, hurriedly pulling on her red leather outfit. "Somehow, Lord Rahl, 'thank you' hardly touches it. You told me to be strong and hold on for you and you would take care of me. You were as good as your word. You always are.

"I find what you did impossible to understand and hard to believe. It also makes me appreciate not only life, but the bond, more than ever before and in ways I never did before."

She gestured to her sisters of the Agiel after pulling a red leather sleeve up her arm. "We have all been to the cusp before, but this was different. This was seeing the threads of life, as you put it. I've seen the Grace drawn before, but when we were there, you showed it to me within myself." She searched for words. "You touched my soul. I now understand your bond to each of us as never before. You are the magic against magic. I am honored to be back in the world of life so that I can be the steel against steel for you and the Mother Confessor."

Berdine stood and helped tighten and buckle some of the straps on Vika's outfit. "For today," she said to Vika, "it's all right with me for you to be Lord Rahl's favorite."

Richard shook his head with a smile. "I don't have favorites. I love you all the same."

"I understand that, now," Vika said with a nod.

"Don't pay any attention to him," Berdine told Vika, ignoring Richard. "He says that all the time. It's not true. For today, you deserve to be his favorite for hanging on to life so you could be here to help us all."

"Richard," Kahlan said, eager to get back to the important matter at hand, "Michec is still down here somewhere. We need to find him."

Richard agreed with a nod as he stood and slid his sword back into its scabbard. "Let's go."

14

They all moved cautiously through the eerie green light and the still, hazy trailers of smoke left from the fire that consumed Michec's underworld minions. Those long, hanging tendrils of smoke swirled around them as they made their way among the forest of corpses and the stench of the dead, eager to be away from the place.

"While you were still in the underworld," Kahlan told Richard from close behind him, "Michec conjured demons that nearly killed us all."

Richard paused at the opening out into the hallway and looked back at her. "I know. I saw the prophecy that he was going to do that. He has the power to somehow open the veil just enough to pull some of those things into the world of life to do his bidding."

"Wait." Shale stepped closer, her hackles up again. "What do you mean, you 'saw the prophecy that he was going to do that'? You said there is no more prophecy. I have been able to see into the flow of time my whole life. Now I can't. While I'm not at all happy about it, you said it is because you had to end prophecy to save the world of life."

Richard leaned out and peered both ways down the hall as far as the visibility from light spheres in brackets on the walls would allow.

"Well, while for all practical purposes that's true," Richard said when he pulled his head back from the edge of the opening, "it's not technically accurate that I ended prophecy. Prophecy is an underworld property and as such it was harmful being here in the world of life, so I sent it back to the underworld where it belongs. In so doing, it ended prophecy in this world, the world of life. But prophecy still exists in the underworld. It can't be destroyed. It's a functional part of the underworld. Think of it as an elemental part of eternity playing out every possible outcome as events branch into the future."

The more he talked, the more Shale's agitation seemed to bubble up. "Yes, I know, the flow of time and all of its many tributaries that I used to be able to tap into. But if you banished it, how were you able to see it and how could you possibly use it?"

"I'm the one who sent it back to the underworld. I was just in the underworld. See what I mean?"

Shale was still frowning. "No."

Richard took a patient breath. "Because I was there, in the underworld, where it exists, I had access to prophecy. So, among other things, I took advantage of it while I was there. Since I'm the one who sent it home, it has a certain . . . familiarity with me."

"Oh, so now it's alive?"

"It's complicated."

Shale cocked her head. "But you used it?" The way she said it made it sound as if she thought that quite unfair, considering that she no longer could. "You used prophecy?"

"Yes, that's right. Prophecy is frequently misunderstood." He turned back to lean toward her a little with an intimidating look. "Even among witch women. I'm a war wizard.

Part of my gift is prophecy. That means I can understand prophecy in ways that no other, including witch women, could ever begin to comprehend.

"So, while there, I took the opportunity to access it. When I did, I found a prophecy flowing out of present events that revealed that Michee was going to open the veil enough to pull some of those underworld beings into the world of life.

"I could see that it was a forked prophecy—a this-or-that type. I knew I had to act to block the wrong fork or you would all die. So, when he pulled them through, I was ready."

Kahlan grabbed a handful of his shirtsleeve. "You were ready? What does that mean?"

"It means that when he fulfilled the first part of the prophecy and pulled those creatures through into this world, at the appropriate moment, I was able to shift it to the alternate fork by blasting them back to where they came from."

"That was the fire?" Berdine asked as she leaned forward in rapt attention. "You blasted those things apart from the underworld? You burned them to ashes?"

Richard nodded. "Sorry I couldn't have been quicker. It was rather . . . difficult to do from where I was at the time."

"But how?" Berdine asked, caught up in the story. "I mean, if you were there, how could you do that here?"

"The Grace," he said. "Everything is connected through the Grace. Those creatures were the souls of evil people. But they had once been created through the spark of life that is the Grace. I used that interconnection of everything in order to destroy their existence in this world where they don't belong. In much the same as I used my ability from there to heal Vika, here."

"If you could do that," Shale asked, folding her arms as if she had caught him in a mistake, "then why couldn't you simply come back through the breach in the veil that Michec created."

"I could have." Richard sighed. "But then I wouldn't have been able to destroy those things and you all could easily have been killed. I had to make a choice—return to fight them and maybe end up having us all be killed, or destroy those things in the world of life before they killed you all. Had I chosen to come back to fight them, the prophecy was not favorable. So, I did what I was sure would work.

"In the end, I was able to do both things, destroy those things and return, because Kahlan thought of a means to show me the way home again. She gave me a path back. It was a much better path than the one Michee had created. His was ugly. Hers was profoundly beautiful."

After checking the hallway again, Richard motioned to the rest of them. "Come on. We have to catch up with Michee. Everyone keep your eyes open. There is no telling where he could be hiding or what he might try to do."

"The goddess sent a horde of Glee," Kahlan said into the silence of the dimly lit hallway. "Shale got rid of them by conjuring snakes." She realized it sounded like she was tattling on the sorceress. Maybe she was.

Richard looked back with a frown. "Really? How?" he asked the witch woman.

"Ah," Shale said with a sly smile, "so now you want to know how I did something that you don't understand and can't do?"

"That's right. I would very much like to know how you could do such a thing. It sounds extremely useful. So, how did you make snakes appear?" Richard asked as he gestured ahead, indicating they were going to need to take the hallway that forked to the right.

Shale shrugged, looking rather smug about it. "I thought them into existence."

Richard paused at the next, dark intersection of stone passageways, bringing them all to a halt again so he could look in both directions. "You thought them into existence?" He turned back to her. "How does that work?"

"I am daughter to a witch woman. As a witch woman myself, I can bring thoughts into physical reality by breaching the separation between thought and reality."

Richard was the one who now looked astonished. "You mean to say that you can think things into existence? It's not just an illusion of something, like snakes? They are real?"

"In a way. Those things we bring into reality, because they are a physical manifestation of our thoughts, are in a way part of us. Because of that, they are also in that way connected to us."

Richard was still staring at her. "But I still don't get how you can make thoughts real."

Shale shrugged again, but this time looking earnest. "Remember when you said that a plan for building the People's Palace and the complication was a way to make the spell-form real? The results of that plan, or spell form, depend on how you draw it, with how many rooms, how many floors, and so on. In other words, the plan is thought, the building follows the thought into reality."

"That's incredible," Richard said, looking genuinely fascinated.

"Not so incredible. At least not to me. You seem to have breached the veil between the world of the living and the world of the dead—now that is incredible. A witch's ability is to breach the veil, you might say, but only between thought and reality. If we can think it, in certain case, we can make it real."

Kahlan remembered all too well those snakes Shale brought into reality. It gave her shivers just thinking about the slithering mass of vipers. She had another thought.

"So then, those vipers the witch woman Shota put on me before could really have killed me?"

Shale gave Kahlan a hard look. "Absolutely."

Kahlan took a deep breath at the thought. "If it's something you can do, then why did you collapse at the end. Were you simply exhausted from the effort?"

"Partly," Shale said as they all started down the dark hallway once more.

She looked uneasy about the question, but when Kahlan keep staring at her, she went on. "When we think something into being, as I said, it is in a way part of us. It is a creation of thought, our thought, and in that way still connected to us. You could even say it remains an integral part of us."

"So?" Kahlan asked as she watched Richard pick a light sphere up out of a bracket and hold it out ahead as he poked his head into a room to the right.

Shale gave Kahlan a troubled look. "I didn't recall those thoughts. They were taken away."

Richard looked back over his shoulder. "What?"

Shale licked her lips with a troubled look. "The snakes attacked the Glee. They were killing them. That was what I intended, why I thought them into existence because I knew they could be deadly. Since the Glee can somehow vanish back into their own world, I knew the danger of doing such a thing. But I only had an instant to do something. It was the only way I could think to stop them before we were all killed."

Richard's brow lifted as he smiled. "In other words, it was an act of desperation?"

Shale nodded unhappily as they started out again. "I guess you could put it that way."

"So what's the danger part?" Kahlan pressed.

"Well, the problem was, once they were attacked, many of the Glee began to vanish back to their home world, the fangs of many of the snakes, now creatures that existed, holding fast onto them. When they vanished, they took those snakes with them."

Richard stopped and turned back. "Why is that a problem?"

"Once I think them into existence, they act according to their nature. They do what the real creature would do. In this case they viciously attacked what I consciously thought of as their prey. In a way, they are real creatures, yet they aren't. Because they were conjured from my thoughts, they acted according to my will. Ordinarily I would simply withdraw the thought that brought them into existence, and they would cease to exist.

"But because there were so many Glee, I had to react out of desperation. I conjured hundreds of them, all at once, and because the snakes were attacking, doing what they do by their nature, they were on the Glee when many of those monsters went back to their own world. I couldn't withdraw the snakes because there were still Glee coming for us. The Glee that vanished took many of the snakes with them."

Richard shared a look with Kahlan. She knew that he had realized something significant, but she didn't know what. It was a look she was all too familiar with. She knew that if she asked, he wouldn't yet be ready to tell her what he had now realized.

Shale swallowed. "When they were taken away like that, rather than me withdrawing the thought,"—she rubbed her arms—"it feels like something is being ripped out from inside me. It was a rather . . . brutal sensation. That sensation overwhelmed me, and I lost consciousness for a time."

Kahlan glanced over at Richard. "That's when Michec showed up."

"He wanted to humiliate me for only being able to conjure snakes," Shale said. "So he made the snakes vanish and brought those demons up from the underworld to show me his power and superiority."

Richard looked like he just had another thought. "Can you bring anything bigger and more frightening than snakes into existence?"

"It isn't big and scary that matters," Shale admonished. "What matters is what works."

Richard let out a sigh as he started them all moving ahead again. "That's true enough."

"The snakes worked," Shale said. "They did as I intended. They kept the Glee from slaughtering us—from slaughtering your two children."

Richard nodded his appreciation as he moved into the darkness ahead.

Kahlan put a hand on the back of Shale's shoulder in appreciation for what she had done, even at great cost to herself.

15

Richard cautiously followed a long, curved passageway, watching for anything out of the ordinary as things ahead gradually materialized out of the darkness. In some places the passageway ascended a half-dozen steps beyond stone columns holding up barreled ceilings that denoted more important sections of the spell-form. In some of those places ornate decorations meant to indicate dominant and subordinate flows of magic within the spell-form had been carved into the stone walls.

Along the way Richard checked each room they came to, leaning back and pushing closed doors open with a foot. While he did find long-dead, mummified corpses in a few, there was no sign of the witch man in any of them. He didn't expect to find Michee in any of those rooms, but he still had to check them just in case.

"Do you know where we're going?" Cassia asked in a whisper that seemed appropriate in such sinister, ornate passageways.

Richard simply nodded as he kept going.

At regular intervals massive stone archways separated sections of what was an important element of the spell form from less significant supporting elements. In places those elements and thus the archways and sections of passageways could be quite complex, reflecting the intricacy of the complication itself.

It still felt disorienting to him to be back in the world of life. Solid ground was hard to get accustomed to again. He had begun to fear that he would be forever imprisoned in the underworld. He cherished the memory, though, of seeing the light of Kahlan's soul when he had been in that dark world. It was a wondrous thing that was like seeing the light of her love for him visualized.

But now that he was back, even that memory seemed very dreamlike and distant. It was just as well those memories faded away since such a place was best forgotten.

As they passed under another soaring archway with columns of gray stone carved into ornamental spiral forms, it opened into a broad room with eight sides. A column in each corner supported a rib holding up the complex vaulted ceiling. On each of the other seven walls before them there was a stone archway just like the one they had entered under.

"Lord Rahl," Vika said in a quiet voice that betrayed her concern, "Moravaska Michec captured all of us. You know what happened then. If we're going after him, well, I mean, what good will it do? Aren't you worried that he will simply capture us again? He likes to play with his captives, but this time I don't think he will make that same mistake again before he kills you and the Mother Confessor."

"I hate to admit it," Kahlan said as she leaned in closer, "but Vika is right. He already had us all once and it seemed effortless. If we catch up with him, he might just as easily have us all in his clutches again."

Richard looked to all the worried faces. "Do any of you know the mistake we made?"

The Mord-Sith all shook their heads. Kahlan bit her lower lip. She didn't have an answer either.

"Sure," Shale said. "The mistake we made was coming down here after him in the first place when we should have been on our way to the Keep."

Richard smiled. "No. The Mord-Sith know what we did wrong, don't you?" he asked them.

They all looked puzzled.

"What happens," he asked them, "when someone tries to use magic against you?"

They all huffed as if it were a silly question.

"If they were foolish enough to do that, then we would capture them by the very magic they tried to use against us," Nyda said.

"Michee is no Mord-Sith," Cassia objected.

"No, he's not," Richard said. He looked from one to the next. "What is he, then?"

Rikka shrugged. "A witch man."

Richard shook his head. He gestured to Nyda. "What is he?"

Nyda shrugged. "Like Rikka says, he's a witch man."

Richard shook his head again. "No. Berdine, what is he?"

She made a face. "He's a bastard witch man."

Richard smiled then looked at Vale. "What is he?"

She lifted her hands out in frustration. "He is called the butcher?"

Richard finally looked at Vika.

"Think, Vika," Richard said. "What is he?"

She frowned in thought as she shared a long look with him. Finally her eyes lit with understanding. "Michec is a trainer of Mord-Sith. When I encountered him up at the stables, I immediately tried to use my Agiel on him. That was my mistake. It was over in that instant. He had me. That was how he did it."

"That's what happened to me!" Berdine said. The others nodded that they, too, had tried to use their Agiel against him.

Richard snapped his fingers. "Exactly. In order to train Mord-Sith, Darken Rahl must have instilled in him the same power instilled into a young woman when she is initiated into the sisterhood of the Mord-Sith. They are given power, through the bond, to use a person's magic against them to capture them.

"I once made the mistake of trying to use the magic of my sword against a Mord-Sith. I made that same mistake again when I tried to use my sword against Michee. He captured me the same way Denna did the first time I tried it."

Shale looked a bit sheepish. "I tried to use magic to stop him as well."

Kahlan was frowning. "I don't remember what happened, but I guess I must have tried to use my ability against him. Used against a Mord-Sith, that would be a very bad death. So why didn't my power work against him?"

Richard looked at her with a sad smile. "He isn't a Mord-Sith. He is a witch man and Darken Rahl gave him the ability to capture those with magic. I'm afraid that I made the same mistake as the rest of you."

Kahlan let out a heavy sigh. "That's how he had us all."

Richard's gaze passed over them all. "So don't make that same mistake again."

"I cut him with my knife," Vika said. "Since that's not magic, he couldn't capture me again. Now he's wounded. So we can hurt him, just not with our Agiel or with your magic."

"Exactly," Richard said. "Using your knife was the right thing to do. But now he's a wounded animal. Now that we understand what his trick was, remember not to try to use your Agiel on him. If you get the chance, use your knives. But that shouldn't be necessary. I will take care of him."

"Not with your sword," Kahlan admonished in alarm.

"No, not my sword. But I will take care of him."

"Lord Rahl," Vika said with a serious look, "promise me that you will let me cut him."

He looked into the iron in her eyes. "You got it."

He had a sudden thought and looked at Shale. "Can you use your ability as a witch woman, not to make something come into existence, but to make something go out of existence?"

Shale looked confused. "What do you mean?"

Richard gestured at the stone column they were standing beside. "Well, for example, could you make this column, or this wall, cease to exist? Make them disappear?"

Shale made a face like he must be crazy. "Of course not."

Richard let out a disappointed sigh. "That's a shame. All right." He gestured into the eight-sided room. "He went down one of the other seven corridors leading out of here. Which hallway did he take?"

Shale's dark expression returned. "How am I supposed to know?"

"You said you could smell a witch. Smell the air at each archway entrance and see if you can smell which one he took."

The dark look left Shale's face. She blinked. "Oh. That's a good idea, actually."

Richard smiled. "And here you thought I was crazy."

Shale smirked. "Not entirely. Just somewhat."

They all followed as Shale started around the large room, pausing in the entryways to sniff the air. She stopped at the fifth archway she came to and spent some time smelling the air. Finally she lifted an arm, pointing.

"He went this way."

16

Following the corridor from the octagonal room, they came to a complex of passageways. Leaning in a little to look into each of them, Richard saw no light spheres. He knew all too well that there were few places as dark as it was underground. Except, of course, the underworld. But that was an entirely different kind of darkness.

In their situation, light wasn't just safety, it was life, so when Shale pointed and before venturing into the blackness of the opening to the far left, Richard lifted one of the glowing glass spheres from a bracket and took it with him. Each of the Mord-Sith followed his example. Together the group of spheres cast a warm yellowish light a good ways into the distance.

Shale tilted her head toward the first narrow hall to the left. "This way. I can smell the witch man."

Berdine looked bewildered. "I don't smell anything other than dust and dankness. What does he smell like?"

Shale gave her a look like it should be obvious. "He smells like a witch."

"Ah. That makes sense." Berdine turned her face back toward Richard and rolled her eyes.

Now, instead of their Agiel, each of the Mord-Sith had a knife in her fist. While Mord-Sith were formidable enough with an Agiel, years of training made them more than a little dangerous with a blade. They knew how to cut a person both to cause pain, to cripple, and to bring a swift death, and they weren't timid about doing either.

Richard didn't want to dissuade them from keeping knives in hand, but he knew that it wasn't time yet. The witch man was still quite a distance away and moving quickly. Soon enough he would go to ground.

Kahlan didn't have her knife out, but from time to time she rested her palm on its hilt, making sure it was still there. Shale did the same.

Richard had never seen the sorceress draw her knife, but he suspected she was just as talented with it as she was at so many other things. For that matter, he sometimes thought she could wound with a look.

Richard didn't bother with his knife. He wasn't going to use it.

At each room they encountered, one of the Mord-Sith, holding a light sphere in her free hand, slipped in to check for the elusive Moravaska Michec. They had no luck. Richard knew they wouldn't but he let them check anyway because it was easier and faster than an argument or having to explain.

"The smell of him is getting stronger," Shale told them. "We're getting closer to him."

Rikka and Cassia took that news seriously and went out ahead to check in the darkness.

"All I smell is dust and dampness," Berdine said to no one in particular.

Richard didn't bother to tell the Mord-Sith to stay behind. They would likely have ignored the order, and besides, he knew that while Shale said they were closer, they weren't yet close enough.

Michec had spent years down in the complication. He had trapped people in it, he had kept them prisoner in it, he had turned victims loose in it so he could hunt them. As a result, he knew the place like the back of his hand. Fortunately, because Richard had spent time studying the drawings Edward Harris had shown them, he had a map of the complication in his head and was able to know exactly where they were. He could envision all of the intersections and passageways ahead of them.

Besides knowing the corridors, Richard understood how the wounded witch man thought, the choices he would likely make, and why. As they came to branching passageways, he knew other things as well, and made sure they went the right way. Shale confirmed his conviction at each of the intersections he took without asking her.

In some places they came to large rooms they had to pass through. Those were secondary nodes in the spell-form. Some had smaller rooms off to the sides. He knew Michec wasn't in any of them, and for the sake of safety from other dangers, he wouldn't let the Mord-Sith check them. It took a look from him for the Mord-Sith to follow his order and stay out of those rooms.

The witch man was leading them through the most dangerous parts of the complication, hoping they would venture into an ancillary node, the way Kahlan and Shale had dived into a room without a floor that had turned out to be filled with water. Richard didn't want the Mord-Sith running into trouble by entering places he knew were dangerous, but not necessarily why. When the Mord-Sith again wanted to check, Richard had to reassure them that Michec had gone on ahead, and not to look in those places because they had dangerous magic. Mord-Sith didn't want anything to do with magic and so didn't argue.

Because he knew the place so well from the plans, Richard knew that Michec was trying to draw them into a trap. Because the man was wounded from Vika cutting him, he would want to get to a place that would give him an advantage. He would want a place that could help him surprise them and trap them with magic. Richard worried about what kind of magic Michec had at his disposal.

For those reasons and more, Richard knew that the witch man was deliberately heading for a complex dead end. He didn't really need

Shale's nose to tell him which route Michec was taking, but he let her point out the correct choices at each intersection or cross corridor they encountered. Each time she confirmed what he suspected, it further narrowed down the possible outcomes toward the one he had believed from the first.

With Kahlan being pregnant with the twins, Richard didn't at all like the idea of taking chances. She had lost their first child. If she lost the twins because they went after the witch man, Richard would never forgive himself. Even so, he knew that the bigger risk was in leaving Michec for some other day. In a way, that was the mistake the witch man had made by leaving Richard alive.

While Richard already knew a great deal about what lay ahead, there was no telling precisely what Michec might be able to do, or what harm he might be able to cause. At the same time, they didn't really have a choice. It was either try to surprise and fight Michec now, on Richard's terms, or fight him later at a time of Michec's choosing and after he had recovered. He might be a dangerous wounded animal, but he was also a weakened animal, so their best chance was to go after him before he could recover.

When they came to a place with four closely placed openings into dark passageways at one side of a spacious room, and one passageway on the opposite side, Shale immediately started for the far-right opening of the four.

Richard reached out and grabbed her arm. "Not that way."

She shot a puzzled look back over her shoulder. "But I can smell that he went this way."

"Don't stand in the opening, yet." Richard guided her to the passageway to the left of the one she had been about to take. "We are going to need to go this way."

"Why wouldn't you want to follow him? We've been following him all this way. If you really want to catch him, he went that way. Why stop now?"

"Because that's a special kind of dead end. It's a twinned spiral. It's a deadly part of the constructed spell-form. He intends to use it against us, and trap us in there."

17

Shale looked even more bewildered. "What do you mean, he intends to trap us in there? How do you know this?"

Rather than answer the sorceress, Richard turned to Vika. "I need you to do something for me."

Vika pulled her braid forward over her shoulder and held it in one fist as she nodded eagerly. "Yes, Lord Rahl?"

"You need to do exactly as I say."

She added a confused look to Shale's. "All right. What do you need me to do?"

Richard gestured, pointing a thumb back over his shoulder at the opening beside the one Michec had taken. "I'm going after Michec down this way."

"But Shale said he took the other passageway."

"I know what Shale said." He pointed, then, across the broad room to another corridor by itself. "I need you to go down that way."

After she looked back over her shoulder to where he had pointed, her expression turned dark. "You promised me I could cut him."

Richard nodded. "And I meant it. Until then, if we are to have a chance, you need to listen to me, and do exactly as I say."

Vika pulled both leather sleeves down tighter as she considered for a moment. "All right, I'm listening."

No Mord-Sith would ever have dared to hesitate at any order Darken Rahl, or any of his predecessors, gave them. To do so would have meant a swift death. Richard, on the other hand, was pleased that Vika had hesitated. It was just another indication that she was beginning to think for herself.

"Go down that passageway, there, until it forks," he said, waggling his hand across the room. "When you get there, take the left fork. A short time later you will come to a steel door. Behind it is another major node. Remember the one we crossed before? The one with the stone bridge?"

Vika nodded. "The bridge that collapsed."

"That's right. Go through that door, cross the bridge and through the steel door on the other side—"

"Is this bridge going to fall in, too?"

"No. At least, I don't think so. Now listen. You need to go through the second steel door on the other side, then take the hallway to the left at the first intersection you come to. Go past two wooden doors on the right side of the hall, then take the next hallway to the right immediately after the second door, go to the fourth wall bracket with a light sphere—"

"What if there aren't any light spheres? Some of these passageways don't have them."

Richard shook his head as he waved his hand for her to be quiet and listen. "There will be light spheres. At the fourth light sphere, take it out of its bracket and throw it on down the hallway as far as you can."

She blinked, not sure she had heard him correctly. "If I do that, it will be pitch black."

"That's right. After you throw the sphere, then turn back and stand there in the darkness."

Vika leaned toward him, confused by the strange order. "Stand in the darkness. Just stand there?"

"Yes. Facing the way you came from, take one pace from the center of that hallway toward your left. Keep your knife in your right hand. Then wait."

The Mord-Sith leaned in a little more toward him. "Wait. All right. Wait for what?"

"You'll know when it happens."

"But you promised me that I would—"

"Vika! You need to follow my instructions exactly!"

She straightened at his sudden tone. "Yes, Lord Rahl."

"Do you remember it all?"

"I think so."

"There can be no thinking so. You must remember it exactly and follow every bit of it as I laid it out. Repeat it back to me. And hurry, we don't have much time."

"Much time for what?" Shale interrupted.

Kahlan hushed her. Shale pressed her lips tight with a look of dissatisfaction as she crossed her arms and remained silent.

Vika looked from Shale back to Richard. She

gestured behind. "Take this passageway to the fork. Take the left fork to the steel door. Go through the steel door, cross the bridge, and then go through the steel door on the other side. Take the left hallway at the second—"

"First," he corrected, holding up a finger. "Take the left hallway at the first intersection you come to."

Vika was nodding, trying to commit it to memory. "The left hallway at the *first* intersection. Then go past two wooden doors on the right side of the hall. Take the next right immediately after the second door, go to the fourth light sphere, take it out of the bracket and throw it as far as I can down the hallway, then turn back and stand there in the darkness."

"That's right. Then what?" he asked her.

"Facing the way I came, I'm to take one step to my left, then wait. Oh yes, and hold my knife at the ready in my right hand."

"Good." Richard grabbed her by her shoulders. "Now repeat it back to me again. You have to get it right, Vika. If you take a wrong turn down here we'll likely never find you. If you take a wrong turn you will die all alone like all the dried-up corpses we've found down here.

I suppose that would be better than dying old and toothless in bed, but dead is still dead."

Vika smiled that he knew what Mord-Sith always said was their worst fear. Then she nodded as she looked up at him and repeated the instructions. She hesitated in a few places. Once she finished, Richard made her repeat it again, then another time until he was sure she had every turn correct.

Shale's suspicion was clearly evident in her expression. "How do you know all this? How do you know all these places, these corridors, and where these turns are?"

"I studied the plans of this place, remember?"

"Yes, but that doesn't explain how—"

"We don't have time to discuss this," he said, cutting her off and letting her know by his tone that he wanted her to stop asking him questions.

"What about your promise that I could cut him?" Vika asked. "Why can't I go with you so that I can—"

"Do you think I would lie to you?"

That made her blink. "No, Lord Rahl."

"Good, because I wouldn't. Now get going. We don't have much time. Hurry, but don't run or you might make a mistake."

After a brief look at her sisters of the Agiel, she turned and rushed off on her mission, her red leather quickly vanishing in the dim distance down the passageway.

Richard turned back to the suspicious sorceress. "I need you to think something into existence."

Startled by the unexpected request, Shale cocked her head. "What do you want me to think up?"

"Something that will distract Michec. Something that will throw him off. Maybe even scare him."

"I told you. He isn't afraid of snakes."

"I didn't say snakes. I said something to distract him and hopefully scare him."

"I don't know that I can conjure something big and scary enough to worry a witch man."

"You told me that it isn't big and scary that matters. What matters is what works. That's what we need: something that works. I need you to think up something that will get Michec's attention. Alarm him. Something that will distract him—distract and hopefully frighten him. If you can make him scream and frantic to get away that would be perfect."

Shale looked on the verge of panic. She lifted her arms and let them flop down at her sides.

"And how in the world do you suggest I do that!"

"Use your head, Shale. It will come to you when you need it. I know it will. I trust you. Now, I need you to go about three dozen paces down the next passageway over, the one he went down, but no closer—I don't want him to know you're in there—then set loose whatever it is you can conjure and send it on down the rest of the way to attack him. After you do that, come back here to this passageway and come after us as fast as you can. I may need you to help with something else. I'm not sure yet."

Shale stood staring at him with her jaw hanging. "You're not sure, yet," she repeated in astonishment.

"We're wasting what little time we have," he told her. "We can't let this opportunity slip away. We may never get another. Get over there, count your heartbeats until you get to a hundred, then do what I asked. Conjure something formidable and send it on down the hall, then hurry over here to us." Richard turned to the others before Shale could object or argue. "The rest of you, come with me."

Richard left Shale to do as instructed as he led Kahlan and the five remaining Mord-Sith to rush into the twin to the spiraled passageway Michee had taken in order to trap them.

18

Richard brought Kahlan and the five Mord-Sith to a halt. Before any of them could speak, he crossed his lips with a finger.

"If you must speak, do it quietly."

Kahlan glanced over at the wall. "Michec is on the other side?"

"Yes."

"Then what are we doing here?" Kahlan asked. "Shouldn't we be over there if we hope to catch him? How do you hope to get him from here?"

Richard smiled. "Wait. You'll see. And remember, don't try to use your power on him. Get your knife out. I doubt you will get the chance to stab him just yet, but you need to be ready in case."

He turned to the stone wall separating the passageway they were in from its twin where the witch man lurked, waiting to capture them. He looked to the right, to the stone pillar not far away, and then to the one to the left, to judge his relative place between them.

"What are you looking for?" Kahlan asked as she watched.

"I don't have time to explain it. Just watch."

Once he was sure he was in the correct spot, as the six women watched, Richard put his fingertips lightly against the wall and slid them over the stone, looking for the right place. When he found the joint between the stone blocks he was looking for, a joint deeper than the others, he followed it to a similarly deep vertical joint and then went to one knee as he followed that one down. In the silence as the others watched him, he traced all the joints at that area of the wall, making sure they were the ones he needed, and being certain of their layout.

Once he was sure he had found the right place and he was sure of the arrangement of the individual blocks, he turned to the women watching him. "As soon as Shale does what I told her, we're going to go through here and try to catch Michec off guard."

Berdine's nose wrinkled in disbelief. "How are we going to get through a solid stone wall?"

Instead of wasting time answering, Richard took hold of Nyda's arm and pulled her closer to the wall. He squatted down, drawing her down with him. He looked into her blue eyes to make sure she was paying attention. When he was sure she was, he traced a stone block about knee height, showing it to her. It was square, each side about as long as his forearm.

"When I tell you, I want you to side-kick this stone block."

She looked at him with a wary expression. "And what am I to do once I break my ankle?"

Richard shook his head. "Don't worry. I'm going to fracture key places in the wall first to weaken everything. It's beveled to balance where it is, so when the rest of the wall comes apart and you kick it, it will be enough to tip it and cause it to give way. It won't take a great deal of force, so you don't have to worry about hurting yourself.

"This block is a critical structural element, but I can't take care of all the right places by myself. I'm going to need you to take care of this one. Once I fracture the wall, freeing it from the stone above, and then you kick it, that block will tip and will fall through and the rest of the wall will come falling down."

He looked at her and then the others to make sure they were all paying attention. They were all more than merely paying attention. They were mystified.

"All of you, be sure to stay clear and get back—especially you, Nyda—once the stone blocks start collapsing. I know the wall is going to come down, but I don't know where all the stone blocks will fall. Many of them are heavy and could severely injure or even kill you if they fall on you. We can't risk that, so be sure to stay clear."

As they were all trying to comprehend what he told them, Richard drew his sword. He tried to draw it slowly enough that it wouldn't make a sound Michec could hear. Still, the unique, high-pitched ringing sound the blade made coming out was almost painful as the magic answered his call. Richard winced as the sound reverberated through the hall, hoping it wasn't so loud that it could be heard on the other side of the stone wall.

Once the sound died out Richard put his ear close and listened for anything from Michec. When he heard nothing but silence, he placed the point of the blade at a key joint low on the wall, and then he waited, listening for the right time.

Kahlan leaned in, unable to stand the tension any longer. "Richard," she whispered, "what are we waiting for?"

He lifted a finger for her to wait as he heard Shale's footsteps in the distance as she came running.

As soon as he heard Michec scream over on the other side of the wall, he said, "That."

Gritting his teeth with the effort, Richard put all his weight against both hands on the hilt and shoved the sword through the low joint between two of the stones. The stone grated against the blade as it slid in. Once it was through, with all his might he pulled the sword upward. Stone popped and shattered, sending small bits flying. After he had cut as far as needed, he pulled the blade back out of the joint.

He could hear Michec, on the other side of the wall, curse and yell. Between angry curses, he let out short screams. As the witch man was struggling with whatever Shale had thought into existence and set upon him, Richard used the hilt of the sword to tap the stone blocks. As soon as he heard a hollow sound that confirmed the loss of integrity, he sheathed the sword.

He looked at Nyda. "Wait until I hit the wall and then kick that stone."

Nyda gave him a single nod. Richard took a step back and, hoping he was right, threw himself at the wall, grunting with mighty effort. As soon as his shoulder hit the stone with his full weight behind it, he could feel the blocks under his shoulder give. Joints popped and shattered as blocks began to tip. As stone started coming apart, he looked back at Nyda.

"Now!"

Nyda threw a swift kick at the stone block he had shown her.

With a cracking sound the stone gave way as if it had no strength at all. Nyda leaped back out of the way. As the wall caved in, Richard almost fell in with it. He regained his balance and jumped back just in time as blocks of stone and broken chunks of rock came crashing down with a rumbling sound. A great cloud of dust billowed up. All of them coughed out dust.

As soon as enough of the stones had collapsed, Richard dove through, toppling a few blocks out of his way to make the opening larger. Some of the stone blocks crashed down to the sides while several others tumbled in ahead of him. He could sense the Mord-Sith charging through right after him. Even as he was going through, more stones, having lost their support, toppled over. Some of the big blocks of stone hit the floor and shattered, sending fragments sliding underfoot.

Richard charged through the rolling clouds of dust. As he emerged on the other side, he spotted Michec. The man looked shocked by the wall collapsing right next to him, and even more so by Richard and the Mord-Sith suddenly storming in at him.

But the shock of seeing them was only secondary to the witch man's plight. What had him in a real panic was the cloud of angry wasps swarming around his face. He was frantically swinging his arms, swatting at them, and trying to swipe dozens of them off his face as they were stinging him. His face was already a mass of angry red welts. His eyes were nearly swollen shut.

Shale and Kahlan came through the dust cloud, both with knives at the ready. With the wasps swarming around his head, Michec took in all the people coming for him with knives.

He immediately turned and raced away, swatting at the wasps as he ran. Richard heard him laugh even as the wasps were stinging his face. Richard knew why the man was laughing. It was the reason he had been waiting in this particular trap of a dead end that delighted him.

Instead of going after Michec, Richard grabbed Kahlan's arm and tossed her behind him, in the direction Michec had run.

"Something very bad is about to happen," he said as he turned to her. "Go. All of you. Go."

"What's about to happen?" Shale demanded.

"Go! I need you all out of the way!"

All of a sudden, a sound Richard had heard too many times before filled the passageway behind him.

Glee shrieked with rage as they came racing out from far off down around the spiraled end of the trap. Hundreds of them filled the corridor. Their screams echoed off the stone walls. Steam rising from their wet bodies rolled along the ceiling.

He knew that the Glee, with their long, muscular legs, could outrun them and would love nothing more than to run down their prey. Running would be the death of them.

19

The slimy, dark creatures were packed into the corridor so tightly they were jostling each other and having trouble scrambling forward as fast as they wanted. Many of them were clambering to go over the top of others so they could be the first to get at Richard, Kahlan, and the rest of them. Richard knew that as much as they wanted them all, they were especially keen to get their claws into Kahlan.

He had no intention of running, but he needed the rest of those with him to get out of harm's way. Looking over his shoulder, he saw them all hesitate.

Needle-sharp teeth snapped. Long arms flailed. Claws reached and raked the air as they shrieked their bloodlust to get at them.

Richard waved his arms at the others, urging them to get back. Not only did he want to make sure the Glee didn't get to Kahlan, he needed all of them back out of the way.

"Go! Run!"

As Shale and Kahlan hesitantly turned to run in the same direction Michec had gone, the Mord-Sith swept in to surround Kahlan. He saw that, at last, they were all running.

Richard turned back to face the enemy racing toward him from around the spiraled end of the corridor where they had been hiding. There were so many of them they were in each other's way and having trouble going as fast as they wanted. Richard hoped that delay would give him the time he needed.

The shrill, angry sound of the steel coming out made Kahlan and the rest of them all stop and turn back to see what he meant to do. They all knew that there had to be hundreds of Glee coming, far too many for him to fight.

Richard looked back over his shoulder. "Keep going!"

They all backed away, none of them willing to leave Richard to fight the threat alone. They didn't realize that he had known that Michec had the Glee hiding back in the spiral, and he didn't have time to explain his intentions to them.

He was worried that they were going to interfere. "Don't stop! Keep going!"

Shale flung her hands out, sending a shimmering wave of light slamming into the mass of the enemy. The arms of several were blown off by Shale's power. That blast of magic ripped straight through maybe a dozen dark bodies before it dissipated. Although it cut down some of the Glee, it was insignificant in relation to their numbers. The mass of the monsters simply ran right over the top of the fallen dead.

"Stop!" Richard yelled back at Shale. "You're going to hit me. I need room! Leave this to me and get back!"

When she nodded her understanding and he was sure that she wasn't going to do it again and accidentally kill him, he turned back, hoping he hadn't lost what little time he had. He needed to act before the shrieking creatures got to him.

Richard turned to the side and took a mighty swing with the sword. The tip of the blade whistled through the dank air. With all his power behind it, he sent the blade crashing through one of the fat columns on the side of the corridor opposite the hole he had created. The massive capital, with its support column abruptly gone, dropped straight down to the floor and shattered, sending shards of stone flying.

Even as some of the stone of the column was still toppling, he rushed to take out the next fat column. As soon as a powerful strike from his sword had shattered the second stone support on that side of the corridor, he rushed to the wall beside the jagged hole he had made. With several more swings, he took down the supporting columns on one side of that opening and then on the other side.

Because the wall had been compromised, it caused yet more stone to drop down. Both capitals fell and rolled back down the corridor toward the Glee. The whole area filled with thick, choking stone dust. He could see that it covered some of the wet, leading Glee in the dense pack coming for him, turning them from black to gray.

After that brief look, Richard turned and started running, arms spread wide, ushering the others, who had only gone a short distance, out ahead, urging them to hurry.

"Why would you do that?" Kahlan asked, confused as to why he would waste the time to take out a pair of columns on each side of the corridor.

"Something I learned in the underworld."

She cast a look back over her shoulder at him as she ran. "What?"

"Keep going. Provided I was quick enough, you'll see."

And then he heard the painfully piercing, distinctive sound of massive blocks of granite cracking. It made a ripping, crackling sound something like rolling thunder but higher-pitched as the fractures raced through the stone, making a popping sound as they went.

Richard couldn't help slowing down to turn and look. He had to be sure. If it didn't work, they were going to be in a lot of trouble. Everyone else stopped with him to look behind.

Back down the corridor, with the key support elements of the fat columns suddenly shattered, the huge ceiling blocks of stone, as wide as the corridor, had nothing to hold them up. All at once they began to fall free. The sound was horrific, and despite their desire to get away, Richard and the others all stood transfixed by the astounding sight.

The closest block came crashing down first, crushing the leading Glee. Blood and gore shot out from under the block as it hit the stone floor. A few arms, their reaching claws still twitching, stuck out from under the immense block of granite that only an instant before had been the ceiling of the corridor.

As soon as that first massive ceiling block had started falling free, the second, with its support now gone, immediately broke loose and started coming down, then the third, then the fourth, and then each of the rest of the ceiling blocks all the way back through the spiraled dead end came crashing down in swift succession.

That dead end became a killing field as the massive blocks of stone, each as wide as the corridor and nearly as thick, plummeted down with a thunderous sound in a series of deafening booms that reverberated through the passageways. The whole place shook with jolt after jolt as the massive granite blocks came to ground, each crushing the Glee packed into the hall on back into the spiral.

It all happened so suddenly and so swiftly that Richard doubted any of the Glee had enough time to vanish back to their own world. He was pretty sure that every single one of them had been crushed to death instantly as the ceiling of the entire corridor crashed down on top of them. He almost felt sorry for them. Almost.

Kahlan stood in stunned silence beside him, looking at the massive block of stone that now completely filled the corridor, blocking off what had once been beyond. The corridor now had a new dead end, one much closer. Clouds of dust that had been forced out from under the blocks as they fell now filled the passageway, some of it still swirling through the dimly lit air.

The Mord-Sith stared in awe at what had just happened.

Shale turned to him. "How did—"

"Come on," Richard said, cutting her off. She looked like a thousand questions were bottled up inside her. "We can discuss it later. Right now we need to catch Michec. Stay behind me."

With that, Richard pushed his way through the knot of Mord-Sith and raced out ahead of all of them.

20

Richard needed to be the one to get to the witch man first. He realized, though, that even while Michec was already injured and now being tormented by wasps, he was still profoundly dangerous. The biggest worry was that Richard had no idea what the man was capable of in spite of his condition. He was aware that they could easily get caught up in a trap they weren't expecting, so they had to be on the lookout for things that they weren't expecting.

Richard only knew that he needed to kill him before he could use any of his dark talents. He especially needed to kill the man before he could harm Kahlan. And, with the Glee showing up everywhere more frequently all the time, they needed to be done with the witch man so they could get to the Keep.

Richard sprinted down halls and corridors, watching for anything unexpected as he took turns instinctively from the mental map in his head and also from his knowledge of where the witch man was headed. Eager to get at Michec, Richard didn't wait for the others, and had soon pulled out a substantial lead over the rest of them. Checking back over his shoulder from time to time, he made sure not to get too far ahead of them lest they lose sight of him and not know which way he went.

If any of them fell behind and made a wrong turn down in the confusing maze of the complication, it could easily be fatal. He just wanted to stay far enough ahead that Kahlan and the others wouldn't fall into the witch man's grasp before Richard could get his hands on the man.

Richard was well aware that Michec was running in a blind panic, taking the swarm of wasps with him, running haphazardly, taking turns at random but still intent on where he was going. He simply wanted to get to a place of safety. That was fine with Richard, because despite the witch man's random course he knew where Michec would end up. Every once in a while, he could hear Michec in the distance, crying out and cursing as the wasps stung a particularly tender spot on his face.

Richard slowed a little to let the others get a bit closer. His blood was up and he wanted to get to the witch man, but he didn't want to let his anger cause him to run out too far ahead and have the others lose sight of him. He looked back over his shoulder at Shale as he ran.

"Those are your wasps, right?"

Shale nodded.

Richard gestured to let them know his intended direction before he cut down a narrow hallway to the right. "Why isn't he simply making them vanish? Kahlan said he made the snake you conjured vanish."

Shale ran up closer to him so she could speak without having to yell. "Because I intended the snakes for the Glee. I didn't know that I needed to shield them against a witch man's magic. I shielded the wasps, though. And, I made sure they were plenty angry. Only I can withdraw them."

Richard slid to a halt and looked up a set of

broad stairs to the left. It was a shortcut that would gain distance on Michec, but it would take them away from his route for a time. He knew that was risky, because Michec, in his distracted state from the wasps, might deviate in his route and end up going someplace Richard wasn't expecting. But he needed to get to Michec before he could escape. The shortcut was the best way to help close the gap.

Decision made, he started up the stairs two at a time.

"When we get close to him," he called back over his shoulder to Shale, "I need you to withdraw the wasps so they don't sting us as well."

Shale nodded as she ran up the stairs after him. "Don't worry about the wasps. I'll make sure they're gone as soon as we catch him."

At the top of the short flight of stairs, a corridor branched off to each side. Richard paused to make sure Kahlan wasn't lagging behind. She wasn't. The Mord-Sith were surrounding her. Reassured, he went straight on down the dark center corridor between the other two. After a short distance the corridor came to stairs that descended back to the original level, where he again took a right.

As he raced down a corridor with dusty marble columns supporting a barreled, plastered ceiling, he slowed and turned as he trotted backward so he could see all the others.

"What magic is Michec liable to use against me when I catch him? Any guesses?"

Shale turned her palms up. "I've been asking myself that same question. I don't have an answer. I don't really know anything about witch men, except that they are witches. That's bad enough, but from what I've seen so far, I suspect he can do things I can't even begin to imagine."

"Do you think you will be able to do anything to counter whatever magic he might do?"

Shale shook her head as she hurried along. "He can't make my wasps vanish. There are limitations for a witch using their power against another witch, which limits what I can do. He is likely to shield anything he does so I can't stop it. You're a wizard, why don't you do something?"

Richard sighed unhappily. "All right. I will just have to deal with whatever he does, if I can't kill him first. But I need you to be ready to at least create light. Conjure a flame in your palm or something—I don't care, but I will need light to see. It's going to be pitch black when I catch him."

Shale blinked in surprise. "How do you know that?"

"Prophecy," Kahlan told her. "Richard was in the underworld, remember? There is prophecy in the underworld. Do you think a war wizard would fail to avail himself of any opportunity to gain an advantage against an enemy?"

Richard grinned at her in answer. He thought she was not only the most intelligent person he knew, but sometimes it seemed she could read his thoughts.

Shale looked alarmed. "You mean to say you have been acting on prophecy?"

"How do you think I knew that spiral corridor was packed with Glee waiting to ambush us? Would you rather I knew nothing about it and walked into Michec's trap?"

"Well, no," she admitted.

As he went past the second wooden door on the right and slowed down, he hushed her before she could ask any more questions.

"From now on," he told them all in a low voice, "try to move as quietly as you can.

Michec won't be far ahead, now. He is down this passageway here, to the right. Rikka, Vale, Cassia, Nyda, Berdine, be ready to use your knives on him to protect Kahlan. Shale, be ready to provide light."

They all nodded as they started out after him down the hallway to the right. As they went farther in, the first light sphere began to brighten, showing them the way. As it was dimming behind them on their way past, the second began to glow. Richard slowed to a stop.

He held up a hand for everyone to be still as he listened into the dark distance. When he heard the echo of heavy breathing, he started running as fast and quietly as he could. He motioned for the others to stay back a ways. He didn't want Michec to snatch Kahlan or anyone else and use them as a hostage. Kahlan had a knife and knew how to use it, but he didn't want it to come to that. The witch man was unpredictable, had magic, and, after all, had called all those Glee back in the spiraled corridor to lay a trap for them.

As the second light sphere dimmed in the distance behind, they hurried past the third, and then beyond, on into darkness.

21

Richard had to judge the distance to the bracket where the fourth light sphere would be by counting his paces between the previous brackets. He began to smell the witch man even though he couldn't see him. He didn't know what a witch was supposed to smell like, but a big man sweating from running and from fear and panic was a smell Richard had no trouble recognizing.

He moved forward a little on his tiptoes. Before he had gone far, as he listened for the wasps and the heavy breathing, trying to judge the exact distance, a big hand came out of nowhere and backhanded him, knocking him back several steps. The surprise, more than anything, knocked him off balance.

Richard immediately regained his footing and dove in the direction of where he now knew Michec was standing. As he crashed into the man, he managed to get an arm around his neck. Michec twisted and struggled to break away. Richard reached up and gripped the wrist of the arm he had around Michec's neck and then used it to help increase the pressure. He knew it would be only moments until the blood supply was cut off to cause unconsciousness.

"Shale! Light!"

All of a sudden, the walls to each side ignited in flame.

In the bright light of the leaping flames, Richard saw Vika standing right in front of them, knife in her right hand.

"Now!" he yelled at her.

As Richard struggled to hang on to the brawny man trying to wrestle his way out of the choke hold, Vika slammed her blade into the witch man's belly. She grabbed the hilt with both hands and grunted with the effort of pulling it sideways, ripping him open.

Vika pulled the blade back and then thrust her left hand into the gaping wound. She pulled her bloody hand back out holding a fistful of entrails. She twisted her body to yank out a long, glistening length of intestine. Michec gasped with the shock of what had just happened.

The corridor suddenly lit with a blindingly bright flash of white-hot light that ignited around the witch man. Richard and Vika both were thrown back, slammed into the flaming wall. They landed on their backs and slid a short distance across the floor back up the corridor. It felt to Richard like they had been struck by lightning.

Richard and Vika both were momentarily stunned by the shock of the blast. Every nerve in his body rang with pain. Richard rolled to his side, his arms going numb. He was blinded by the intensity of the flash.

Michec, lit by the wavering flames of the walls, glared down at them both. He started to draw his hands up. Richard suspected he was going to fry them with another lightninglike strike. He knew that if he did, it could kill both him and Vika.

Despite the pain, Richard forced himself to jump to his feet, and without an instant's delay he crashed into Michec, grabbing him with both hands around his throat. The full force of the impact threw Michec's arms back, stopping him from what he had been just about to do to them. Richard knew that he couldn't allow the man to gather his wits and his power or it would all be over.

With all his might he rammed the big man into the wall. He gritted his teeth with a growl as he used all of his strength to lean in and force Michec's head back into the flames. Richard could smell the witch man's spiky hair burning. Michec reacted to the pain of the fire by thrashing wildly, trying to get away, but Richard held him tight as he used all his strength to choke the life out of him. His muscles bulged with the effort.

Something as thick as his leg whipped around Richard's middle and forcefully yanked him back. Despite his best effort, he couldn't hold on. Richard saw the red leather of some of the other Mord-Sith charging in for Michec, but another blindingly bright flash of light threw them back to land at Kahlan's and Shale's feet.

As Richard was dragged back, with the thick thing squeezing the air out of him, he thought that it had to be a tentacle of some sort, like the one he and Kahlan had fought in the water. He couldn't see its source. He put his hands on it to try to push it away and found that it wasn't soft, like living tissue, but rough and hard, like a rapidly expanding tree root.

As he twisted his body, trying to get away from its grasp, he saw yet more of the tendrils sprouting up out of the floor, breaking the stone apart as they rose up, growing fatter as they rose up. Before he was able to do anything about the one tightening painfully around his middle, another, lengthening and curling as it grew up out of the floor, coiled around his legs. Yet another rose up to grab his arms.

The rootlike tendrils grew in thickness and strength as they threw yet more coils around his arms and legs. He looked over and saw that the same kind of tendrils were climbing up Vika, thickening rapidly as they encased her, squeezing the air from her lungs.

Michec panted, trying to recover his strength. Wisps of smoke rose from his singed hair and the back of his robes. A long length of bloody intestine hung down to the floor. Blood from the gash soaked his filthy robes and began to puddle around his feet.

He grabbed hold of the intestine in his fist, and with a flash of knifelike light from his other hand severed it and cast the length aside as if it was no longer needed. He lifted a hand out to each wall, and the flames started to dim as the fire rapidly began to extinguish.

Michec turned to Vika. "Seems you made the same mistake you warned me of. Trying to teach a lesson of revenge rather than simply killing me. I am no longer going to bother with lessons for any of you. I'm just going to kill you all."

Suddenly, the corridor shimmered as a wave of light shot through the air. Richard could no longer move his head, but he could turn his eyes just enough to see Shale, Kahlan, and the rest of the Mord-Sith running in to help. The wavering light hit Michec, staggering him, but it failed to do any visible damage. He took a few steps back as he regained his balance and his senses.

Richard could feel the roots around his chest constricting. Every time he breathed out, they tightened, taking up the extra space, so that he couldn't get his full breath back. Each time he exhaled, it ratcheted him another notch toward suffocation. He tried panting with shallow breaths, but even those were being squeezed out of him.

Michec cast a grim look over the people trying to kill him and then lifted an arm. When he did, it brought up a wall of fire of his own. The searing flames blocked the advance of the women. Pleased that it drove them back, Michec turned and hurried off down the corridor, disappearing into the darkness.

The roots that had Richard and were growing thicker by the moment had finally cut off his air. His vision narrowed to a pinpoint of light in the center of blackness. He could hear Vika also struggling unsuccessfully to breathe.

A flash shower of rain came out of nowhere and dumped buckets' worth of water in the corridor, extinguishing the fire that Michec had used to block the others from coming after him.

Kahlan, Shale, and all the Mord-Sith raced to Richard.

"Hold on," Kahlan said as she frantically started sawing away with her knife at the roots and vines that had encased him.

Out of the corner of his eye he could see the red leather of a few of the others rushing over to try to help Vika.

"I can't use magic on this," Shale said as she desperately cut at the roots with her knife. "I can feel that Michec shielded them and his magic can overcome whatever I try to do. We have to do it with our knives. Hold on."

Kahlan gritted her teeth as she furiously cut through a thick root. Fortunately, it was relatively soft, rather than woody, and she was finally able to sever it, releasing the pressure and allowing him to at last draw a breath. His vision started to return from the blackness. He gasped air, angry at himself that he had let this happen.

It took some time before Richard and Vika were finally cut free enough that they were able to untangle themselves from the network of fibrous tendrils.

Once back on his feet, Richard lifted the sword a few inches and let it drop back, making sure the scabbard hadn't been bent or crushed and that he would still be able to draw it.

"Michec is pretty badly wounded," Richard managed to say between deep breaths. He winked at Vika. "Vika managed to hurt him more than I did."

Vika smiled her appreciation that he had kept his promise to let her cut him good.

"Vika has lived up to the honor as your favorite for today," Berdine said.

Richard wanted to respond but didn't feel up it right then.

"We need to go after Michee," he said instead. "I want to kill him in case he doesn't bleed to death. Is everyone all right?"

A quick glance revealed nods all around.

"All right, then, let's go."

22

"Look," Rikka said, pointing. "Blood. And I can see more out ahead."

"There's quite a lot of it, too," Cassia said as she leaned down, taking a better look. "That will certainly make it easier to follow him. At some point it should start slowing him down, too."

Richard thought about it briefly and then turned back to Shale. "You can conjure things. So can you conjure blood?"

Shale frowned a little as she considered the question. "I've never thought about it before, but now that you ask, I imagine so. If nothing else, I could conjure a pretty good imitation of it."

"Go ahead and try." Richard gestured down

at the long drizzle of blood on the stone floor. "See if you can make a blood trail that looks like that one."

Shale lifted her hands, her fingers wavering as she closed her eyes a moment in concentration. A wet swath of blood appeared on the floor, looking very much like the splash beside it that Rikka had found.

"Like that?" she asked as her eyes came open and she dropped her arms.

"Yes, that's good."

"Obviously," Shale said, "you are suggesting that the trail of blood may be a trick?"

Richard put a hand on his hip as he tried to put himself in Michee's place and think what he would be likely to do. "We have to assume that it's a possibility. He's wounded. He doesn't want to have to fight us right now. He would want to divert us until he can deal with his injuries. The best way to do that would be to lead us into a trap. There are certainly plenty of those down here."

"You mean like the spiraled dead end."

Richard nodded to the sorceress.

"How did you know that you could bring the ceiling down like that?" Shale asked, finally getting back to the question she had been burning to ask.

"When I studied the plans, I saw it there. The plans were drawn so that such a trap would be constructed when the place was originally built. The way it was constructed, that ceiling was designed to fall to either trap or crush people. You just had to know how to initiate the trap. When I studied those plans, I could see how the trap could be triggered. It wasn't too hard. You just had to know the weak spot."

Shale arched an incriminating eyebrow. "And did you also see the Glee hiding back in there on those same plans?"

"Of course not," Richard said, waving a hand dismissively. "I saw that in a prophecy while I was in the underworld."

"Ah. Again a prophecy." She gestured for him to continue. "And what else did you see?"

"I saw a prophecy that revealed where Michec would go. That's why I had Vika go there and wait—so that she could stab him just as the prophecy said she would."

"Then why wasn't he killed right there and then?" Kahlan asked. "If it was in the prophecy, why didn't it end right there as the prophecy said?"

Richard let out an unhappy sigh. "Because it was a forked prophecy. I saw that he would go to that spot, Vika would stab him, then we would either kill him or, if events took a less likely turn down the other fork, he would escape. Unfortunately, we are in a complication. A complication has an effect and it can twist events in prophecy.

"It fell the wrong way for us and events in that prophecy ended up taking the other fork. That fork was less clear and soon ends without resolution. Forks in prophecy often aren't always resolved in the particular prophecy where the first fork occurs. If it takes one of those secondary forks, then you need to find another prophecy that picks up where that particular fork left off. That's often the problem with prophecy."

"So then, on the fork in which he escaped, where does he go next?" She looked off down the passageway, as if she might chance to see him. "When and where will we be able to catch him? Could you at least tell that much?"

Richard wiped a hand over his mouth. "That particular prophecy ended either with his death, or his escape down the other fork, but that prophecy didn't go down that secondary fork. I would have to look for the next prophecy in the chronology to hope to be able to reestablish the event line and tell where he went after he took the fork in which he escaped. I didn't do that because once prophecy starts forking, the possibilities multiply exponentially."

Kahlan gave him a dark look. "If you're thinking of returning to the world of the dead so you can look for that prophecy, you can just forget it. These two children need their father."

Richard flashed her a reassuring smile. "No, I promise you on my word as a wizard, I have no desire or intention of returning to the underworld to look for that prophecy."

Kahlan leaned in and gave him a quick kiss on the cheek. "That's my boy."

"So what do we do now?" Shale asked. "Follow this blood trail, or assume it's a trick?"

Richard put a hand back on his hip, staring down the corridor, thinking. He at last turned to her.

"Send your wasps after him again. Let's see where they go."

Shale looked off into the darkness. "I can do that, but we won't be able to follow them for long. They fly fast."

"Let's see if we can follow them long enough to see if they follow the blood or take a different route."

"How are you going to have the wasps follow him if you don't know where he is or which way he went?" Berdine asked.

Shale's mouth widened with a sly smile. "Wasps have an excellent sense of smell. I will give them his scent and they will find him."

"All right, good," Richard said. "Send them."

Shale again lifted her hands and waggled her fingers.

She opened her eyes. "Done."

Richard looked off down the hall and saw where the buzzing swarm appeared and headed off down the corridor.

"Come on," he said as he started running. "We need to keep sight of them as long as possible."

23

"Just as I thought," Richard said as he came to a stop when he saw the swarm of wasps flow around a corner to swoop down and disappear in a low, round passageway made of brick. He gestured ahead, then to the round opening at the side. "The blood trail goes that way, but the wasps went down here. The blood was a trick."

Vika leaned down, looking into the circular passageway where the wasps had gone. "There aren't any light spheres in this tube. We'll need to get some and take them with us."

Taking her cue, the rest of the Mord-Sith raced up the hall, and each lifted a glass sphere from a bracket and brought it back.

"What is this place, anyway?" Kahlan asked

as she leaned down a little so she wouldn't hit her head as she peered into the dark, brick pipe. "It doesn't look like anything else we've seen down here."

"The complication is a low place beneath the People's Palace." Richard gestured off into the pipe she was peering into. "This is the lowest place in the complication. Water seeks the lowest level. This is an emergency drainage shaft in case there is ever torrential rain and the water manages to overwhelm the drainage system up above and flood all the way down here. This pipe drains the complication if needed."

"That makes sense for water," Kahlan said, "but why would Michec go this way?"

"He's injured. I think he went in here to hide."

"How can he hide in this shaft? It's round. There's no place for him to conceal himself."

Richard glanced over at her. "He's counting on us believing that. I've seen the plans. I know better."

Before entering the round passage, Richard looked over at Shale. "Don't forget, we can't directly use magic on the witch man, even when he is wounded. He has already proven that. But when you sent wasps after him, he wasn't able to capture you."

"I think that's because I wasn't using magic against him, as I did the first time. I created angry wasps with a desire to attack. I wasn't personally attacking him directly."

"That seems like a questionable exception," Kahlan said. "Are you sure he can't turn your magic back on you like the first time?"

Shale pressed her lips tight a bit as she considered briefly. "No, no I don't think so. The first time was a direct attack. The use of the wasps and the fire I made on the walls to each side of the passageway so Richard could see were tangential. Because they were indirect, that broke the link back to me. It doesn't give him a direct route to return to the source, namely me, with his own power."

"I hate magic," Berdine muttered. "It makes no sense."

Richard flashed her a brief smile and nod of agreement before he turned to the others. "We all survived back there because there were nine of us, and together we are stronger. We can't directly use magic, but there is strength in all of us together. Remember that if we can find him."

Like everyone else, Richard had to bend at the waist to be able to fit into the drainage pipe. Berdine, being the shortest, only had to tip her head to the forward a little in order to fit. Because the drainage shaft was round, and they were crouched over, they had to use their hands on the brick at the side from time to time to keep their balance. As they went farther in, the round shaft started going downhill in a gentle slope in order to drain the water.

In places water from above seeped through a series of round weep-holes in small blocks of stone set into the brick and accumulated at the bottom. The farther they went, the deeper the flowing water became, but it never reached more than ankle deep and since it was moving rather than stagnant it didn't stink. When they came to side drains that emptied into the main drain they were in, Richard stopped.

"Which way?" Vika asked.

Richard thought through the plans in his mind. He looked back at all the faces watching him in the eerie light of the glass spheres.

"We need to get to the low point. This way, straight ahead."

"Couldn't you be wrong about where he would have gone?" Shale asked. "For some reason I can't pick up his smell anymore. Couldn't he have gone off down one of these pipes to the sides?"

"Of course," Richard said without looking back as he started out again. He noticed dead wasps floating in the water.

"Then he may be planning ahead and instead of going where you think he is, he could be lurking in one of those side drains and be waiting for us in the darkness."

Richard looked back over his shoulder but didn't say anything as he kept going. He knew she was right, but he had a gut feeling born of growing up tracking wounded animals. He thought that he knew where Michec would have gone to ground.

After moving through the drainage pipe for a time, he turned back again and crossed a finger over his lips.

"We're close," he whispered. "Try to move as quietly as possible."

He cautiously led them ahead until they

reached a square opening in the floor of the drain tunnel. Water that was draining along the pipe from both directions cascaded over the edge and down into the darkness. He was glad to hear the sound it made, because it would help cover any sound they might make.

Richard leaned toward the others, holding out his arms to gather them all in close so they could hear him. "This is the place. I think he's down in there."

Kahlan glanced over at the square opening. "What is this opening?"

"Any water that makes it down here drains into this rock drain."

"But what is it?" Kahlan asked.

"It's a massive pit filled with crushed rock. At the sides, near the top, it has a number of small pipes leading to the edge of the plateau in case there is ever too much water for the rock drain to hold. Unless it's a huge flood, the rock pit will hold all the water and let it slowly dissipate without damaging the foundation."

Shale craned her neck to look over at the dark opening. "What makes you think Michee would have gone down there?"

"Because he's an animal. Animals go to ground when they're injured. They instinctively seek out a hole to hide in. It makes them feel safer."

Shale looked skeptical. "Michec may be a beast, but he is also a person who is able to think. More than that, he's a cunning person. People act differently than animals. You are just guessing that he's down there hiding in a hole. He may be long gone."

Richard bent over and scooped up some dead wasps. He held them up before her as he lifted an eyebrow.

Shale stared unhappily at the dead wasps, and then looked around, noticing that there were many more all over the floor. "Making conjured snakes vanish is one thing. They weren't shielded. Killing conjured things that are shielded is altogether different. I can't even begin to guess at his abilities and how dangerous he is."

"How far down to the bottom?" Kahlan asked.

"There would be no reason for the top of the rock to be down deep in the pit. I believe the rock should come up pretty high. I doubt we could all stand up straight down in there."

"Why not just let him bleed out?" Kahlan asked. "Why risk going in after him?"

"Because Shale said he just did something he shouldn't be able to do." Richard gave Kahlan a sympathetic look. "I'd like nothing more than to simply let him die in misery down there. But for all we know about his abilities he might be able to heal himself enough to survive. He didn't seem concerned about cutting off the length of intestine hanging out of the gash Vika cut in him. We would never know if he managed to survive and would never expect him to come after us another time—until he unexpectedly showed up and killed us."

"If we're going down in there, I think it would be better if the Mother Confessor waited up here," Cassia said. "It would be safer than her going down in there with us."

"And what if I'm wrong?" Richard asked. "What if while we're down in an empty dry pit looking for him, he's really up here somewhere and he sneaks up from behind and murders her?"

The worry showed in Cassia's expression. "There is that."

"The nine of us need to stay together,"

Richard told them. "There is no telling what Michec might do. Besides that, it may take all of us to kill him. Look at what he did with those vines. It took all of us to escape them."

Kahlan turned to Shale. "Would his injuries limit his ability to use magic?"

Shale sighed. "I would like to think so, but since I don't even know how powerful he is when he's healthy, there is no way to be sure how much his injuries would limit his powers. Worse, even if his gift is limited, for all I know it still may be more than enough to kill us all. I think it best if we assume his present abilities are still quite lethal."

"We need to go down there and eliminate him. That's all there is to it," Richard said. "There is supposed to be an iron ladder going down there. Kahlan, after we jump down, you take the ladder."

She started to protest. "But—"

"You're pregnant. If it's a bigger drop than I think, I don't want you to take a bad fall and lose the twins. No unnecessary risks."

"You're right," she said in resignation. "The ladder it is."

Richard gestured around at them all. "The

rest of you gather around the opening and then all jump down with me, all at once. Except you, Cassia. Stay behind and follow Kahlan down to guard her back. Once we're down there, we can't waste time finding him. We need to be quick. The more surprise we have on our side, the better. We don't want to give him time to do something that could stop us."

He looked around until he got nods from everyone. "Enough talk. Let's go."

24

Richard landed hard on both feet, Shale right beside him. Fortunately, it wasn't any farther down than he had thought. All the Mord-Sith, each with a light sphere, landed to the sides. Richard saw Kahlan hurrying down the iron ladder with Cassia right behind her.

Concerned at not seeing the witch man, Richard immediately started looking into the darkness in the distance, trying to spot him. There were simple, square stone posts at regular intervals throughout the expansive pit. The posts held up arches that in turn held up the low ceiling. The loose, ragged rock filling the pit tried to twist his ankles with every step, making it difficult to walk on.

Richard worried that the witch man might have heard them and could be hiding behind one of the massive stone supports, ready to surprise them with a lethal attack.

Without needing orders, the Mord-Sith all immediately started spreading out in an ever-widening circle, going farther into the darkness with their light spheres, searching for the witch man. They checked behind each stone post as they moved swiftly into the distance. Richard didn't want one of them to encounter Michec alone, so he stood ready to react if any of them spotted him.

Vika suddenly cried out and pointed. "There!"

Richard and the others turned and raced across the uneven rock and past several stone posts to catch up with her. As she held up the light sphere, it revealed Michec slumped in shadows of a dark corner like a spider waiting for prey. His robes were soaked in blood from the waist down, but he looked as merciless and menacing as ever. He sat up straighter but didn't try to stand under the low ceiling.

Vika, with a cry of rage, ran in and heaved her light sphere at him as hard as she could. Michec thrust out a hand. The glass sphere shattered explosively in a thousand sparkling shards.

He snarled a curse and flicked a hand toward the Mord-Sith. Vika screamed as a blast exploded the crushed rock she was on. The discharge of his power threw her flying back through the air. Rock flew in every direction.

Most of them had to stoop or duck under beams so as not to hit their heads as they ran toward the corner. As they got closer, Michec lifted his arms out to the sides, his fingers pointing up, and bursts of fire erupted from the floor in front of them. The heat drove some of them back as they shielded their faces with an arm, not just from the flames but also from the flying rocks.

Richard didn't slow. As he ran toward the corner, he dodged around every shower of fire the witch man ignited in his way. The others darted around the roaring columns of flame, trying to keep up with him. Kahlan, not far away, kept pace with him as she, too, wove her way through the sudden explosions of fire. The roaring flames lit the square posts in orange-yellow light. There seemed to be fire flaring up all around. Richard ducked first one way and then another, snaking between posts and fire as he raced for the corner.

Michec suddenly cast his hands out with great force. The rock of the floor blasted up at Kahlan, throwing her through the air to land on her back. Richard's heart felt as if it jumped into his throat at seeing her skid along the jagged stony surface. He saw several of the Mord-Sith thrown back with her in the same explosion of rock.

Richard kept the stone posts and fire between himself and the witch man as best he could to conceal himself as he rapidly closed the distance. When Michec suddenly turned and caught sight of him leaping through a fount of fire, he swung his hands around toward Richard. But it was too late. He was already there.

Richard dove in atop the man, seizing him by the throat.

Gritting his teeth in fury, Richard squeezed with all his might. As he did, the witch man swept both arms up. As Michec lifted his clawed hands, dark, rootlike branches sprouted from the stone walls on each side of the corner. Bony black tendrils grew like skeletal arms from the walls with frightening speed. The fingers of woody vine lengthened to grab Richard's wrists, pulling with powerful, conjured strength.

Mord-Sith dove in on each side. Nyda grabbed one of Michec's arms. Vale fell on top of the arm beside Nyda, helping her push it downward. Berdine fell across his legs to help hold him down. Rikka and Cassia, covered in stone dust, suddenly appeared and dropped onto his other arm, pinning it down so he couldn't lift it higher, but it was already too late. The rootlike tendrils wouldn't let go of Richard's wrists, and in fact grew thicker and pulled with more power. He fought against them, trying to put pressure on Michec's throat.

Vika reached in beside Richard with a knife to cut the witch man's throat above Richard's struggling grip. Before she could get the blade on his throat, a sudden, deafening blast threw her through the air again, this time even farther. She landed quite a distance back. Richard heard her grunt as the air was driven from her lungs when she slammed into a stone post.

Shale, not far behind Richard, lifted her hands, her fingers slowly waggling. When she did, as her eyes slowly rolled up in her head, more of the woody vines sprouted from the stone walls above the ones Michec had conjured, coiling around the ones holding Richard's wrists. Fingerlike branches grew out of the ends of the arms she created and grasped the thick, dark roots that continued to curl around Richard's arms.

Shale, her eyes half closed, worked her fingers. As she did, the rootlike arms she had summoned struggled to pull back on the dark tendrils that had a firm grip on Richard's wrists and forearms, preventing him from crushing Michec's windpipe. Despite Shale's efforts, the vines the witch man had conjured wouldn't let go. Richard's hands shook from the strain of trying to strangle the man against the power trying to pull them back. Yet more vines sprouted from the walls to either side. They were dark in color, like the first ones, so Richard knew that they, too, were the work of the witch man.

In his mind's eye, he remembered the sight of Kahlan hanging by the shackles, her beautiful face bruised and swollen from a beating Michec had given her. He remembered the witch man telling him how after he was finished skinning her, he would let the Glee rip the two babies from her womb while she was still alive.

Those horrific memories fueled his fury as his hands shook with the monumental effort to overcome the woody vines trying to drag his wrists back. Richard screamed with rage as he struggled to choke the life out of the witch man. The tendrils holding him started to crack and come apart. Even as he tried with all his might, and even as he was able to start to break the hold on him, he knew it wasn't going to be enough.

All of those around Richard struggled along with him. He could see the sweat and effort on the faces of each one of the Mord-Sith trying to hold Michec's arms to prevent him from lifting them to call forth even more horrors. When Nyda managed to pull her knife, it suddenly flew from her hand and clattered against a post.

With a cry of effort born of rage, and determined to end it, Richard managed to press in harder on Michec's throat. He could feel his thumbs starting to compress the man's straining muscles.

"Wait!" the witch man cried out. "Lord Rahl—wait. Listen."

Richard didn't answer. He didn't care what Michec had to say. His actions and life had already revealed the truth about the nature of the man. Richard simply wanted him dead.

"I can see now that I was wrong. You really are rightly the Lord Rahl. I can see that now."

Richard struggled all the harder.

"Lord Rahl! I was only following orders!"

Richard didn't dare to waste any strength to ask the man whose orders he was following. To each side, the Mord-Sith grunted with the effort of holding the man's powerful arms. He was so strong that he lifted all four a few inches off the floor.

"I will swear loyalty to you!" the witch man cried out. "I will swear loyalty to your empire! Let me go so I may serve you!"

Richard wanted to tell him that he could serve him best by dying, but he didn't dare spare any effort to speak. Try as he might, with the conjured hands holding his wrists back, he couldn't close his grip enough on the man's throat to crush his windpipe and kill him.

"Let me live and I will serve you just as I served your father. I will protect and serve your wishes! Just let me go and my life will be yours to command. I can be useful to you! Please, Lord Rahl, allow me to serve you!"

In answer, teeth clenched tightly, Richard tried all the harder to crush Michec's windpipe. He could see the Mord-Sith to each side losing their grip as the witch man managed to start to lift his arms and turn his hands up.

25

Richard's muscles burned with exhaustion as he fought against the vines trying to pull his arms away. He knew he wasn't going to be able to hold on much longer. The Mord-Sith to each side were having even worse problems. The danger to all of them increased with the strain of pulling every breath.

Richard should have been able to strangle the man by now. It was obvious that the witch man's powers were somehow energizing him with desperate strength beyond that of a normal man so that he was able to overcome all of their efforts. It was clear that they were all now locked in a struggle to the death.

"Forgive me!" Michec cried out. "I was only following orders!"

Richard glared into Michec's dark eyes as he struggled with all his might to strangle him. His hands shook with the effort. His muscles burned.

Richard didn't want to give the man the satisfaction of asking whose orders, but the witch man told him anyway.

"I was only following the queen's orders!"

Richard didn't know what queen the man could be talking about, but he didn't believe him. Michec would say anything to escape. Richard wondered if maybe he was talking about the Golden Goddess, but she was described as a goddess, not a queen.

Kahlan appeared to the right of Richard, covered with dust from the rock the witch man had blasted up at her, trying to kill her. Blood streamed down her face from several wounds.

A strange look of bemused calm came over the witch man's swollen, red face. "If you think this witch's oath begins and ends with me, you are a fool."

That time, Richard couldn't resist asking, "What are you talking about?"

"Ask your witch," he said with a sneer.

Kahlan suddenly dropped in beside Richard,

using her full weight to drive her blade between two of Michec's ribs and into his heart. She let out of cry of rage as she pivoted the handle of her knife from side to side, slicing through his heart.

Michec's eyes went wide.

Kahlan, gritting her teeth, keeping her knife pressed hilt-deep in his chest, put her face in close to his, looking into his startled eyes.

"Think to harm my babies, do you?" she growled. "I deliver you now into the hands of the Keeper of the underworld. He will take you into darkness you can't begin to imagine. You will never see the light of Creation again. All those innocent souls you tortured to death will now torment you for all eternity."

Michec's mouth worked, trying to beg for mercy, to explain, but no words came forth. The panic and terror in his eyes was clear. He had never had a shred of mercy for the panic and terror of his victims, and now Richard, Kahlan and the others with them had none for him.

Vika, covered in stone dust and with a gash across her forehead that had her face covered in a mask of blood, knelt to Richard's left. Without pause, she rammed her knife into the side of Michec's neck. Blood oozed rather than spurted out from the artery she severed. His heart could no longer pump blood.

The surprise in Michec's eyes slowly faded as the life went out of them until his stare was blank and empty. The bony hands holding Richard's wrists released their grip on him as they crumbled into dust and vapor.

Shale, her eyes still closed, dropped to her knees, clearly drained from the effort of trying to pull back on the vines that had so powerfully held Richard's wrists. Exhausted, she put a hand down on the rock for support.

Finally, Richard sat back on his heels, letting his cramping hands drop to his lap. He looked around to see everyone panting along with him from the effort. Despite being battered, and some of them bleeding, none of them seemed seriously hurt.

He finally circled an arm around Kahlan's neck and pulled her close. He brushed hair back from her face and kissed her forehead, then hugged her tight, grateful that she was alive and not seriously hurt. She took her bloody hand from her knife in Michec's chest and with both arms hugged him back, silently thankful to be alive and have the ordeal over.

At last, after a brief time to hold Kahlan tight, get his breath back, and be thankful that she was safe, Richard finally struggled to his feet. He helped Kahlan stand. All of the Mord-Sith untangled themselves from their grips on the dead man's arms and legs.

"You did it, Lord Rahl," Berdine said as she gazed hatefully down at the dead witch man. "You killed the butcher."

Richard shook his head. "No, we all did. It took all nine of us. The Law of Nines had more power than even a witch man."

The Mord-Sith looked pleased that he included them. Shale, with a hand on her knee to help her stand, managed to show a weary smile along with them.

They all backed away a short distance to stare at the dead man, all of them still having some difficulty believing the monster was finally dead. It had been a monumental struggle, but the witch man would no longer bring terror and pain to anyone.

Spotting something he didn't like, Richard gestured to the bloody body slumped in the corner as he looked over at Shale.

"Burn him to ash, would you please?"

Shale looked a little surprised by the request. “Why? He’s dead. What do you think he can do, now?”

“I don’t know, and I don’t want to find out. You’re good at conjuring fire. Do that now. End it. Burn him to ash.”

Shale turned an uneasy look from Richard, to Michec, and back. She suddenly seemed both distressed and apologetic.

She shook her head. “Lord Rahl, I am a witch woman. I can’t burn another witch. Never. That act has terrible significance.”

Richard felt his anger heating. It made no sense to him.

“Even a man as evil as this?”

She couldn’t seem to look him in the eye, so she stared off at the dead Michec. “I know that he was a monster, but he is also a witch. I wanted him dead just as much as the rest of you, and I helped with that to the best of my ability, but I can’t burn a witch, not even a dead one. I just can’t.”

Richard was surprised, but it was obviously something profoundly personal to her. He wondered why, but rather than asking her he deemed it best not to force the issue.

He laid the palm of his left hand over the hilt of his sword. When he did, he was surprised to feel the magic from the sword stirring, trying to join with him. He surmised it could be that the sword's magic sensed his lingering rage at this evil man and all the horrific acts he had committed.

And then, as Richard looked over at the dead man staring back at him with dead eyes, he saw it again, a glint of something, some spark of light in those dead eyes that shouldn't have been there.

In that instant, he envisioned the horrors starting all over again. He saw everything they had just won suddenly slipping away from them. He saw that threat to Kahlan and their children reawakening, as if Michec were somehow trying to strike out at them one last time from the world of the dead before he would sink away into its eternal darkness.

From somewhere deep within him, without Richard consciously summoning it, the primal rage of his birthright awakened. With his left hand still on the hilt of the sword, drawing on all the ancient power of the weapon, he cast his other hand out, opening his fist, instantly igniting wizard's fire. The rotating bluish-white ball of flame shook the room with a reverberating boom as it exploded into existence. Seemingly at the same instant it came into being, it shot across the room, wailing with a piercing shriek as it lit the stone posts and all the stunned faces on its way to the source of Richard's ire. The sound of it was deafening as it hurtled the short distance to that target and burst apart on impact, splashing sticky fire over the body of the witch man.

Wizard's fire burned with a fierce intensity and purpose unlike any other fire. The roaring flames burned white hot at their center.

Shale wrinkled her nose at the stench of burning flesh. The Mord-Sith didn't.

In mere moments, the soft tissue was consumed in the ferocious blaze. Once the soft tissue had burned away, the wizard's fire continued to sink inward until it covered the bones, engulfing them in the savage flames until they, too, began to break apart and finally turn to ash and collapse into a brightly glowing heap. Only then did the fire, its work done, finally extinguish.

Everyone stood in stunned silence at what they had just witnessed. The heat from the wizard's fire had even partly melted the stone wall behind where Michee had been slumped.

"I didn't know you could do that," Kahlan said in a soft voice as she stared at the aftermath.

Richard felt a bit stunned himself. "Neither did I."

Shale looked shaken by what she had just seen. "I've heard whispered stories of such a thing. I never imagined I would live to see it with my own eyes."

Richard stared at the pile of ash that was all that remained of a henchman for Darken Rahl, a witch man who had been determined to kill them all, glad it was finally over.

The sorceress turned to him with a grave expression. "How did you do it?"

Richard slowly shook his head as he stared at the still-glowing pile of ash and asked her a question instead. "Did you see that glint of light in his eyes?"

Shale was taken aback. "No."

"I have no idea how I did it," he finally told her. "When I saw a spark of light in his dead eyes, I simply acted."

He knew that such an ability would be more than useful against the Glee, but it had all happened in an instant. He had absolutely no idea how he had brought it about.

After a moment of silence, Kahlan circled an arm around his waist. "Can we please get out of this wretched place?"

Richard smiled down at her as he looked into her beautiful green eyes. "Sure."

"We can now safely be on our way to the Wizard's Keep," Shale said, still looking a bit shaken.

"We've been down here an awfully long time," Cassia said. "We need to get some food."

Berdine grinned. "I could eat."

26

On their way out of the vast maze that was the complication, they passed between two columns at the end of the corridor and entered a sizable area with dozens of glass spheres in iron brackets lighting a formal stone floor made of black and white marble squares. The walls had decorative tiles. To each side there were a pair of white marble columns supporting tall arches with ornate carving. Richard knew that although it was a node, this one was a benign junction in the spell-form.

As the group crossed the large area and then passed between the two columns on the opposite side where the corridor continued on, something made Richard lag behind and then look back up over his left shoulder to where he could see through the tall arch to a part of the upper level where it crossed the lower one they were on.

A single Glee stood there in that gallery, looking down, watching. Somehow, Richard had known it would be there.

As the others continued on, carrying with them the soft murmur of conversation, Richard slowed to a stop and stared up at the dark figure. He realized that it hadn't been watching all of them. It had only appeared to watch Richard. Its third eyelid blinked as they stared at each other.

Richard couldn't help simply standing there, looking up at the still figure, the way it stood still looking down at him. He wondered if it could be the same individual he had seen on several previous occasions.

Almost as if in answer to the question in Richard's mind, the Glee bowed its head. Richard was stunned to see it do so. It made no hostile move. It didn't give him any other indication of its intentions, only that single bow, almost as if out of . . . respect.

And then it simply turned to scribbles and vanished back to its own world.

Left standing there staring up at an empty upper level, Richard had absolutely no idea what the sighting could possibly mean, but he felt a deep conviction that it had, in fact, been the same individual he had seen before. Of course, he had no way to know for sure. But if it really was the same one, he had now seen this particular Glee three times. The previous time it had spread its claws to show him that they were webbed. This time, it didn't. It bowed its head instead. On none of those occasions had it shown any sign that it intended to attack.

If anything, Richard felt that on each occasion it had simply been observing him. Each time Richard had spotted the lone Glee, it had been after he had killed large numbers of its kind. And yet it did not try to attack him. This time, though, it showed up after they had killed the witch man. The thought occurred to him that not only was it a witch man, but a witch man who had made some kind of pact with the Golden Goddess.

He wondered if it could be an observer for the Golden Goddess, reporting back on any observed weakness. So far, all it had to report was a lot of dead Glee and now a dead witch.

Another thought occurred to him that ran a chill up his spine. It made him momentarily stop dead.

"Richard?"

He blinked and looked down at the corridor to see Kahlan standing there, turned halfway back, waiting for him.

He immediately trotted to catch up with her. As exhausted as she was, she managed to flash him her special smile. As exhausted as he was, he couldn't help returning a smile, even if he didn't think he could in any way match the radiance of hers. It warmed his heart to see that smile, her beautiful face, the love in her eyes.

He took her hand and hurried to catch up with the others at a shorter archway complex held up by polished but dusty marble pillars to either side. Just beyond were four openings in a wall of rough stone.

"Which way, Lord Rahl?" Vika asked. The gash on her forehead had stopped bleeding, but her face was still a mask of blood. It matched her red leather.

Richard gestured. "The one in the middle."

She looked toward the wall and then frowned

back at him. "There are four openings. There is no middle one."

Richard nodded toward the openings. "Take the second from the right. Once into the darkness where you can't see it yet, it forks. The others don't. That makes five passageways. Take the left fork and that will be the middle one. It's a concealed shortcut."

Vika shook her head. "Only the Lord Rahl could see what no one else can."

"It's not magic. I saw the plans beforehand."

"So did I," Vika said. "All I remember of them is that it was a confusing mess."

"It isn't nearly so confusing for me but only because I understand spell-forms and the language of Creation."

"I hate magic," Berdine muttered.

The rest of the Mord-Sith nodded their fervent agreement.

Richard couldn't help smiling his joy that they had all survived.

"We'll be up and out of here shortly," he told them. "Then we can all get cleaned up. Vika, you can finally wash the blood off your face."

She shrugged her indifference. "I don't mind blood."

"Well, we are going to be up in the palace soon, where there will be other people. Seeing blood on a Mord-Sith in red leather scares people."

"As well it should," Vika said without a hint of humor.

These women were still mad, but he was encouraged that at times they showed glimmers of their humanity. At other times, though, they were simply stone-cold mad.

"What about getting to the Wizard's Keep?" Shale pressed. "The witch man is dead, so we can now safely leave the palace without having to worry about him sabotaging our cause in your absence. We need to be on our way at once. It's not safe for us here. The sooner we leave, the better. We can clean up later."

Richard sighed. "It would probably be best to get something to eat." He glanced at Berdine. She flashed him a smile. "It would also be good to get a proper night's rest."

He hooked a thumb behind his belt as he considered. "But with the extreme danger of the Glee attacking us unexpectedly while we're still here, that would not be the safest thing to do." He tipped his head toward Shale. "You have a good point. If they discover that we're still here, they will continue their attacks. There is no telling how overpowering the next attack might be. We might not be able to stop them the next time. If they win just once, all is lost

"The safest thing to do, the thing that would best protect Kahlan, the twins, and the future of our way of life, would be to do as we first intended when all this started and leave immediately in darkness."

"You mean the plan when Michec captured me?" Vika asked.

Richard nodded. "The threat from Moravaska Michec has been eliminated, but the threat from the Glee most definitely hasn't. We need to get back to our original plan of getting away from here and to the safety of the Keep."

"I think I should be able to gather horses and supplies this time without any nasty surprises," Vika said with a clear tone of relief.

"And I will make sure that we leave unseen so that the Glee won't know where we went," the sorceress said. "That should give us some breathing room."

"It should be well after dark by the time we can get the horses and supplies," Kahlan said.

"While not the best for traveling, leaving in the dark would certainly help us evade any spying eyes."

"Let's get to it, then," Richard said, as he started ahead.

As they finally went through the last of the locked doors, the guards were there to greet them.

"Lord Rahl!" exclaimed the first one to see them. Along with the rest of the men, he stood up straight and tall as he saluted with a fist to his heart.

"I hope everything went well for you?" the man asked.

"We accomplished what we needed to do," Richard said without elaboration, locking the door behind them.

Berdine grinned at the guard. "We killed a witch."

He blinked in shock. "A witch? But how could a witch possibly get in there?"

Richard handed the man the keys Michec had been using. "As it happens, he was also a pickpocket."

27

By the time they made the long walk through the public areas of the palace where they had to worry about being seen by the goddess through the eyes of all the people in the halls, then along the routes hidden from the public where they didn't have to worry about the goddess seeing them, and then they were finally back up at the stables, it was deep in the night. After the ordeal down in the complication, they were all exhausted, but escaping without the Glee knowing that they were gone—or where they had gone—was more important than sleep. They were all eager to make good their escape sight unseen and be on their way.

None of them talked as they waited in hiding up at the stables. They were preoccupied with their own thoughts and no one was much in the mood to talk. They knew they had an ordeal ahead of them and dangers they couldn't yet imagine.

Vika rushed back behind the manure wagon and leaned down. "Everything is ready, Lord Rahl. Horses with supplies are gathered in the staging area. I told them that it was for a distant but routine patrol. I didn't want them to know it was for you."

Richard smiled. "Good thinking, Vika."

"Besides the travel food that will keep, the kitchens had just finished a late-night meal for staff, so I was able to get us some freshly cooked food for when we're able to stop."

Berdine grinned. "I guess you are a favorite to all of us today."

Richard ignored Berdine and looked back over his shoulder at Shale. "All right. Do what you need to do to hide us from the men in the stables so we can leave unseen."

Shale gave him a look that was part witch woman and part sorceress. "What do you think I've been doing? I wanted to make sure we weren't discovered waiting back here. We can go anytime. They won't so much as notice us. Even if the Golden Goddess searches their minds, there will be nothing of us there for her to find or see. We just have to be sure not to linger, lest the spell wear off."

Kahlan leaned in. "Is there anything special we need to do? Anything we need to wait for?"

"No," Shale said as she stood. "We can mount up and be on our way. But the spell won't last long."

The witch woman walked out into the open and past a man headed to one of the stables. The rest of them cautiously followed her toward the waiting horses, feeling more than obvious. Richard looked around as they made their way across the grounds, but none of the stable workers appeared to notice them. They walked right past a man carrying rakes and shovels toward the first building. The man was whistling softly to himself and didn't even look up

When they reached the horses, they all checked the gear, and made sure the saddle girth straps were tight. They tested the security of the saddlebags and the sacks tied to each of the horses. The horses seemed calm. They were used to late-night patrols.

Richard hooked an unstrung bow and a

quiver stuffed with arrows on the back of the saddle of one of the larger horses. When he was finished checking that everything was secure, he moved forward, keeping his hand on the side of the horse so it would know where he was. He spoke softly to it and finally stroked its neck. The horse tossed its head in response, as if to say, "Let's go." It was hard to tell in the weak light of lanterns hanging on the fronts of buildings, but the animal looked black.

Kahlan stroked the nose of the mare right behind, then scratched its forehead. It whinnied softly and nuzzled its head against her in appreciation of her gentle touch.

All of the others made similar quick introductions and, once done, mounted up. They all urged their horses ahead at a quick walk through an arched opening in a nearby inner wall. As they rode, Shale, swaying gently in the saddle in tune with her horse's movements, held her hands out to the sides, palms up. She had already told Richard not to worry, that she wouldn't fall off, that the horse would watch out for her safety. She assured them that it was what she needed to do to be sure that no one saw them.

After they went through the massive gates in

the outer wall, they finally emerged at the road leading down the side of the plateau. The walls of the palace soared overhead. Richard slowed his horse to get closer to the witch woman. Her eyes were closed as she rode with her hands held out to the sides.

"We're starting down, now," he told her as he placed his horse strategically between her and the edge of the cliff.

"I know," she answered, sounding unconcerned.

It made him a bit nervous to see her ride with her eyes closed and not holding on to anything, although her body moved fluidly with the rhythm of the horse's gait. As they made the first switchback turn in the road that wound its way along the nearly sheer walls of the plateau, he looked over the edge, down into the darkness of the Azrith Plain far below.

"It's a long drop. Maybe you should keep your eyes open?"

"The horse knows where it's going," Shale murmured.

"But still . . . don't you want to watch to make sure your horse doesn't, I don't know, ride off the edge in the dark?"

"No. I'm afraid of heights. Better that I don't look."

Richard sighed. "Have it your way. Not much to see in the dark, anyway. But we're going to be at the drawbridge soon. We don't want those men to recognize us."

"Send one of the Mord-Sith ahead to tell the soldiers to lower the bridge for a patrol," Shale instructed. "When we go past them, they will see only soldiers on their way out to patrol. They will not recognize us or remember what we look like."

Richard called Rikka forward and told her to do what Shale said, then he hurried his horse to catch up with Kahlan. Rikka rode out ahead of them to have the soldiers lower the drawbridge. He could see it in the distance, lit by a series of lanterns.

As they rode across it, their horses' hooves clopped over the heavy wooden planks. A few of the men casually tapped a fist to their hearts. It was a greeting to fellow soldiers on their way out on patrol and not at all the more formal way they would have saluted superiors, especially the Lord Rahl. Richard was glad to see by that casual salute that none of the men recognized them.

It wasn't long before they left the lamplight on the bridge far behind. The light from the palace high above them at least showed enough of the road to keep them from stepping off into a dark void.

By the time they reached the bottom of the plateau and the road leveled out onto the flat ground, Richard had finally started to relax a bit. As they rode out onto the Azrith Plain, Shale at last lowered her arms and opened her eyes.

Richard looked back over his shoulder to see the sprawling People's Palace atop the enormous plateau. It seemed to blot out half the sky. Walls, towers, and ramparts rose up impossibly high. Torches, lanterns, and fires lit the palace. That firelight reflected off the low clouds enough to keep the darkness from being total.

While there wasn't light enough to make out much of the features of the flat terrain and sparse vegetation, there was enough for him to see the shadowed shapes of everyone with him atop their horses. He was glad for that little bit of light, because he wanted to make sure that they stayed close together and that none of them accidentally became separated. They needed to stay together.

While the heavy cloud cover did reflect a little light, the farther they went the darker it became out on the vast plain. The only thing he could see well was the glowing palace in the distance behind them. He didn't like riding horses in the dark, because if they happened to step in a hole, they could break a leg, but with the little bit of reflected light off the clouds, he thought it was an acceptable risk and one they had to take, at least until it got too dark to continue.

They kept on riding in silence for a time after the palace was no longer visible behind them. He knew that they all felt a sense of vulnerability out in the flat, open country, but Richard wanted to make absolutely sure that they would be far enough out of sight of anyone up in the palace looking out over the plain, so he kept them moving ahead.

When he was just able to make out some kind of feature ahead of them, some distortion in the ground, he dismounted and had everyone do the same, then walked his horse forward rather than let it ride blindly into possible trouble. As he walked carefully ahead, he could just make out that the ground dropped away into some kind of shallow gully, but he couldn't see it as well as he'd like.

"Shale, can you light a small flame so we can see what this is?"

She handed the reins of her horse into the care of one of the Mord-Sith, and then she came forward. When she lit a small flame above her upturned palm, it was just enough to see the lay of the land. Slightly to the right, the ground slumped away, leading down to the bottom of what looked like a wash worn through dry ground by flash floods.

With Shale providing that small flame for light, they all filed down into the gully.

"This area is low enough that if there is anyone in the surrounding area, they won't be able to see us," he told them.

"Should we look for material for a fire?" Cassia asked.

"No," Richard said. "A fire would reflect off the clouds and reveal our location. Anyone near would also be able to smell the smoke. We can light some travel candles to see by so we can have something to eat. If memory serves me, I think Berdine is hungry."

Everyone laughed.

"Well, I admit," she said, "the aroma of that fried chicken has been driving me crazy."

After they broke out small candles in tin carrying housings, Shale lit them all, and they used the meager light to scout the area. A small stream through the gully bordered with scraggly vegetation and a few clumps of grass provided a place to picket the horses and finally gave them the opportunity to clean up and tend to wounds. The horses had eaten back at the stables only hours before, so Richard decided to save their valuable oats for when needed. After the horses were unsaddled, they munched on what clumps of grass they were able to find.

Once they found a suitable place to sit, they all gathered close together around a few of the travel candles, then eagerly unpacked the food. It was still warm and smelled wonderful.

Richard was well past tired, and he knew the others were as well, but he was hungry.

"We need to set up watches," he told them. There were still dangers to be worried about. "Two people on each watch. That should let us all get a halfway decent sleep."

"There are nine of us," Kahlan said. "How

do you want to manage that uneven division?"

"You're pregnant. You don't need to stand watch. You need the sleep for the twins."

Kahlan opened her mouth, about to protest, but her better judgment apparently got the better of her. She pushed her long hair back over her shoulder. "All right. As tired as I am, I'm not going to argue. Neither are the twins."

Richard smiled to himself at the thought of them. "Vika, you and I can take first watch. Then however the rest of you want to divide up is fine."

They all grunted their agreement as they ate chicken.

"Can you pass me some of that hard cheese?" Kahlan asked.

Richard looked up from his piece of fried chicken. He finished chewing a mouthful and then swallowed.

"I like cheese," he said, "but you hate cheese."

"I know," she said, seemingly unable to explain it, "but for some reason I'm really hungry for cheese."

"Cravings," Shale said with a smile.

Richard looked over at the sorceress. "What?"

Shale gestured with the bones of a chicken wing toward Kahlan. "She's pregnant. She is having cravings."

Richard blinked at the sorceress. "But she hates cheese."

Shale's smile widened. "Well, apparently, at least one of her babies likes it."

28

As dawn broke in the east, they all ate a quick breakfast to finish off the chicken. The low clouds let rays of light through a band of sky at the horizon. The bottoms of the clouds turned pink at first, then gradually a deep purple.

Kahlan was eager to have another piece of cheese. She knew she hated cheese, but for some reason it tasted wonderful. She couldn't explain it. She supposed that Shale was right that at least one of her babies had a taste for it. As she ate it, she rubbed her belly.

"This is for you," she told them.

After they had packed up their bedrolls and gear, they saddled their horses while Vale and Cassia were off on a short scouting patrol to make sure there were no surprises lurking about. One of them went off in each direction to check the gully, since that was the only place where they couldn't see for miles, unlike the rest of the desolate Azrith Plain. It was a quick reconnaissance and they both returned to report seeing nothing and finding no footprints. While many people came to the People's Palace from all over much of D'Hara, in the direction they were headed across the Azrith Plain the land was deserted and there was no civilization before reaching the Midlands.

As Kahlan struggled to lift her saddle up over her mare's back, Richard rushed over to help. Kahlan was strong. It seemed odd to her that she was having trouble lifting her saddle. She decided that with all they had been through down in the complication, the encounter with Michec, and having only a short sleep, she was simply tired.

Richard stepped in beside her, taking the saddle out of her hands. "Here, let me help lift that."

He hoisted the saddle up onto her mare, and she got to put a hand on his back as he pulled the strap underneath and tightened it.

She was glad for the chance to touch him, to feel a connection to him. After all that they had nearly lost, it was reassuring to touch him and see him smile. Though it was going to be a long journey, it would be a joyous one to not only be away from the constant threat of attack but to be with Richard.

She grinned as she looked up into his gray eyes. "We're going to have babies."

He bent and kissed her. "I will always protect them, and you. We'll teach them to be good people. I promised you a golden age and I still intend to keep that promise."

Darkness unexpectedly crept into her thoughts. "What about the Golden Goddess? Maybe you are mistaken and that is the golden age that is coming. She is in another world. How can we possibly defeat her? How can we stop her from coming for our children?"

Richard sighed, his smile fading with the change of subject. He didn't have an answer, so he didn't try to lie to her.

"I promised you I will protect them, and I will."

"I know. You will think of something," she said, forcing cheerfulness into her voice, trying to sound optimistic and bring back his smile. "I know you will."

His smile made a brief reappearance.

She gazed out toward the still-dark horizon to the west after she saw that the others looked like they were about ready to leave. "Which direction?"

Richard took a quick look off into the distance to the dark horizon. "Aydindril is northwest from here as the crow flies. That would be the obvious choice, but with a formidable mountain range lying across the straightest route from here to Aydindril, mountains where the boundary once stood when we were growing up, that's a problem. The boundary may be gone, but these mountains still present a formidable barrier."

Kahlan shuddered at the mention of the boundary. When it had come down, it had unleashed Darken Rahl and the might of D'Hara on the Midlands. It had been the end of a long peace, the end of all the other Confessors, and the beginning of a horrific war. But the boundary coming down had also brought her to be with Richard. The world was so different now, but those mountains reminded her of the way things used to be.

"It's possible we could find a way across those mountains," Richard said, "but if we found a pass, it would be a dangerous crossing. Any high pass across that range would likely mean we would need to abandon the horses at some point. And that's if we can find a such a pass.

"It's also possible we could wander around in those mountains and never find a way across. Much of that range rises thousands of feet in nearly sheer rock walls. While it would theoretically be the shortest distance to Aydindril, I think trying to go that way would mean we would have to go on foot, spend a lot of time only to come to impassable cliffs, and even if we eventually found a way over it would end up taking longer. Not only that, but like I said, if we can find a pass up in those mountains, it's likely to be dangerous."

Kahlan stared off to the west. She knew those mountains, and she knew he was right. "It's the heat of summer down here, but high up in those mountains weather could be a big problem."

He nodded as he checked a saddle strap under the stirrups and then tipped his head more toward the left. "Southwest will get us to the Kern River. There will be a road along the river. It would provide an easier way over into the Midlands. It's longer, but easier traveling and a lot less of a risk."

Kahlan sighed as she looked toward the northwest, toward her home, toward the Confessors' Palace, where she had been born, and where the Wizard's Keep waited. She hadn't realized how much she missed home. Now that they were going to Aydindril, she felt a sense of excitement to get there. The idea of having her children born where she had been born sounded wonderful to her.

"If we go too far south to cross the Kern we will end up in the Wilds." She lifted an eyebrow at him. "You know what that's like."

Richard grimaced as he nodded. "Well, maybe if we spot any possible gaps in the mountain range, we can find a way across long before we have to go that far south."

Kahlan nodded. "And if we can find a way across the mountains before we have to go too far south, we will end up in populated parts of the Midlands, where we can get any supplies we need. That will make our travel easier. Even if we do have to abandon the horses to get across, we can get horses in those lands."

"There is that," he said. "But don't forget, we need to stay out of sight of people as much as possible."

"You're right." Kahlan sighed. "It sounds like for now we need to head southwest through the desolate parts of D'Hara to get beyond at least the largest of the mountains. To the south they aren't as formidable as they are up here to the north."

"We will stay as close to the mountains as practical but still in areas that allow us to make good time. That way, I may be able to find a way over the mountains and into the Midlands sooner rather than later. Once we cross over, we can head north to Aydindril." He smiled at her. "If there is a pass, I'll find it. I am a woods guide, after all."

Kahlan returned the smile. "I guess we have a plan for now."

As eager as she was to get to the Keep, she knew they had to be smart about it. There was a lot of wild and dangerous country between them and where they needed to go.

"Everyone ready?" Richard called out.

Shale climbed up in her saddle after confirming that she was ready. The Mord-Sith mounted up, also letting him know that they were ready. When Kahlan saw Nyda yawn, it made her yawn, too.

In short order they were on their way. They rode up out of the gully and then headed southwest across the featureless plain for the rest of the day. As the sun started to sink off to their right, Kahlan was just able to make out a ragged, pale blue line of mountains in the distance, outlined by the sun as it sank behind them. She guessed those mountains would still be a number of days' ride if they went directly northwest, toward Aydindril, but with the way they were heading to the southwest to skirt the highest of those mountains, it would likely be many days before they were close to the long spine of the mountain range where Richard could start looking for a way over it. The sooner he could find a way, the shorter their journey would be and the sooner they would reach the safety of the Keep.

The frustrating thing was that they were going farther away from Aydindril all the time because the imposing mountain range prevented a more direct route. She told herself it couldn't be helped.

As tired as she was, it made Kahlan feel good to at least be headed home, even if indirectly, and, hopefully, the worry of the Glee would be left behind them.

It excited her to heading home with her two unborn children of D'Hara. She hoped to raise them for a good part of their childhood where she'd grown up, where she had first discovered the excitement of the natural world around her.

As they rode, she couldn't keep her mind from drifting back to thoughts of Michee, when she had been hanging from the manacles as he was about to skin her, and the threat that the Glee were going to rip her babies from her womb.

Unexpectedly, the memory of the glint she had seen in the dead witch man's eyes just before Richard burned him to ash began to haunt her as she rode.

Witches had a way of never letting you feel entirely free of their reach.

29

Kahlan laid the reins down on her horse's neck and then rested her wrists on the saddle horn. She sat quietly, waiting, as Richard stared off at something. They had been riding since first light, and she was getting saddle-sore. As she waited, she put her hands on her sides and stretched in both directions as best she could.

Whatever it was he was staring at had Richard looking troubled, so much so that his behavior was beginning to spook her. She didn't like it when he turned quiet like this. It usually meant trouble.

A light mist tingled against her face, feeling like icy little sparkles. The weather had been gloomy for the past three weeks. Or was it four? The monotony of it was getting to be mind-numbing. Somehow, she felt as if she was losing count of the days as they made their way endlessly through a quiet wood of tall pine and fir on their way southwest.

Soft streamers of hazy light angled down in long shafts among the towering tree trunks, illuminating the veils of mist floating in the occasional breath of gentle breeze. Here and there small stretches of granite ledges broke up through the forest floor. A light fog moved silently among some of the fern beds between the rock outcroppings. The towering canopies of the trees left it somber and deathly quiet down on the forest floor. Because of the perpetual shade, little brush grew, leaving the ground open among the trees.

Down where they were, with the thick canopy so far above them, not even the wind reached them. While it was quiet now, she had on some days heard the distant sound of the wind gusting far above them. Sometimes, in the drizzle, the only sound was water that collected on the pine needles letting go and dripping down to splatter on the large leaves of moose maples. She was tired of huddling under rain gear. It never kept them completely dry, making for miserable travel. She ached for the warmth of sunlight.

Everyone else waited behind Richard and Kahlan as he silently studied something. She was getting impatient.

"You know, for some reason, I feel like I've seen that rock before," Kahlan said to break the silence. She swiped accumulated mist off her brow. As she flicked the water off her finger, she gestured ahead. "That one there, the one that looks like a big nose on the side. It looks familiar."

Richard finally turned a troubled look back toward her. "That's because you have seen it before. This is the third time we've come this way."

Kahlan blinked in disbelief. Richard grew up as a woods guide. The forest had been his home for much of his life. He didn't lose his bearings in the woods.

"How is that possible?"

He turned away toward the rock again. "I don't know."

"What's the problem?" Shale asked from behind them.

Richard stood in the stirrups and looked back

at the others. "Do any of you recognize this place?"

Baffled, Berdine glanced around. "Recognize it? How could we? Trees all look the same. How could we possibly recognize one place from another?"

Nyda looked about. "The woods all look the same to me, too."

The rest of the Mord Sith all nodded their agreement. Mord-Sith weren't exactly familiar with forests, so Kahlan wasn't surprised they thought that trees all looked the same.

"So what's going on?" Shale asked, clearly getting impatient.

Rather than answer her question, he asked her one instead. "What direction are we heading?"

Perplexed, Shale lifted an arm to point out ahead. "Southwest. We've been heading southwest for weeks."

"I don't know a whole lot about the woods," Cassia said, "but I'm pretty good with direction. Shale is right. We've been heading southwest the whole time. Straight as an arrow," she added.

Shale regarded him with a curious look, sensing that something was amiss. "Do you for some reason think differently?"

"No," Richard said, "I agree, we've been heading southwest for a long time."

"So what's the problem?" the sorceress asked.

"The problem is, despite going in the same direction the whole time, straight as an arrow, as Cassia put it, this is at least the third time we've been in this exact same spot. Without a road or path, we are moving randomly among the trees, so even traveling in a big circle we wouldn't necessarily come across the exact same ground. Yet this time we did. If fact, this is the third time we have been in this same place in the woods."

The Mord-Sith, now alert, all looked around. Shale rode her horse forward, closer to Richard and Kahlan.

"What are you talking about? That's impossible."

Richard gestured ahead. "Do you recognize that rock?"

Shale wet her lips as she hesitated. "As a matter of fact, I might. I seem to remember it because it looks like a nose growing out of the left side."

"You mean we've been traveling around in a

big circle?" Vika asked as she rode her horse up on the other side of Richard.

He nodded. "I believe so."

"We can't afford to waste time riding around in circles." Shale was beginning to sound more than a little aggravated, as if she thought he was doing it deliberately. "I thought you were a woodsman, or something."

"Or something." Richard sighed as he laid both wrists over the horn of his saddle. "All I can tell you is that as far as I know, we have been riding southwest for weeks, but this is at least the third time we've come across this rock. That can only mean that we are traveling in circles."

Shale glanced around suspiciously. "Well, have you seen hoof prints from all our horses to confirm your suspicion? If we've been here before, there should be some signs to confirm it."

Richard shook his head unhappily. "No, I haven't. But I know we've been in this spot before. I can't explain it, but I'm telling you, we are somehow going in a circles."

"Maybe it just looks like another rock we saw before," Berdine suggested. "The rocks all have different shapes, but a lot of them are kind of similar-looking—like the trees. Maybe this one only looks similar to ones that you've seen before."

He gestured around at the woods. "Look at the type of forest we're in. It never changes."

Berdine wrinkled up her expression at what he could be talking about. "Of course not. Woods are woods. They all look the same."

"No they don't," Richard said with quiet disagreement. "At least, they shouldn't. As you travel you move into different areas. Vegetation changes. Trees grow different sizes with different soil conditions. Rocks and the terrain change from time to time. Sometimes windfalls will create openings for a meadow, or a tree nursery to spring to life. But the woods we've been in have not changed since about the time we entered them."

"Now that you mention it," Kahlan said, "the woods have been looking pretty much just like this for weeks, now. That is odd. We should be getting somewhere, but it doesn't seem like we are."

Richard nodded. "That's because we are somehow riding in a big circle."

"Well, except for the first day, it has been cloudy and drizzly for the entire time," Vika said. "It has been too overcast to see for sure where the sun is in the sky, and down here, under the cover of trees, it is even harder to tell."

"You're right, but the sun isn't the only way to tell direction," Richard said. "More than that, though, something feels wrong."

Shale squinted at him. "Like what? What are you suggesting?"

Richard sighed as he shook his head. "Maybe it's been too long since I've been in the woods. Maybe my skills have gotten rusty and something is confusing my sense of direction."

Kahlan thought that highly improbable, but she didn't want to say it out loud.

30

After another week of long days of traveling, or maybe it was longer, Kahlan couldn't remember for sure, they again arrived at the same rock that looked like it had a nose on the side of it. This time, though, they were positive it was the same rock, because the last time they had been there Richard had scraped a big X on the side of the nose. When they saw that X again, everyone's heart sank. No one doubted any longer that they were indeed traveling in a big circle, and no one had an explanation, least of all Richard.

The only good thing was that they had seen no other people, although that might have been a welcome relief, and importantly, they had seen no sign of the Glee.

"All right," Richard said, "I don't know how this can be possible. It makes no sense, but it makes less sense to keep doing what clearly isn't working. We have to do something different."

Kahlan could see how frustrated he was. "Like what?"

"There are a number of ways to make sure you are maintaining your direction of travel. The best way is to use landmarks to keep you on course. A prominent ridge or mountain are a good way to keep your bearings. Even high ground can give you sight of some landmark to use, even a distinctive tree. But in these woods, we can't see anything like that. We're going to have to do something else."

Berdine made a face. "What else is there to do then? With the clouds we can't be sure of the direction of the sun. We can't see any kind of landmark except these trees, and they all look the same."

Richard didn't argue the last point. "We are going to have to use plot lines to make sure we are going in a straight line. These woods are fairly open, the ground is relatively flat, and without much vegetation down low we can see for quite a long distance."

"How does that help us?" Vika asked.

"There are nine of us. That is an advantage we can use. We need to spread out in a straight line. When the last person in line can see at least the next two are lined up in a perfectly straight line ahead, then the next person goes out ahead. Guided by hand signals, they will go left or right so that the ones behind can ensure that they are positioned in a straight line and that the people in front of them are always in a direct line of sight. Everyone has to be lined up with at least three people visible ahead to make sure our line is straight.

"Once all of us are strung out in what we know to be a straight line, then the last person in line can go forward and take the lead, with the first few of us in line making sure they are positioned properly on that straight plot line. In that way we keep leapfrogging a line that we know to be straight, and we can keep it straight going forward.

"I don't know what the problem is, but for some reason these woods are confusing us—confusing me—and we aren't traveling in a straight direction. I don't know the cause, but this should solve the problem. It will be slower traveling, at least for a while, but once we get beyond this problem area, we should be able to spot landmarks. When we do, then things will return to normal."

Shale gazed around at the woods as if scrutinizing them for the source of trouble. "Do you think it could be magic of some sort causing this strange aberration?"

"I don't know what the problem is," Richard said. "But by doing this we should be able to get beyond this troublesome area to where we need to be traveling, no matter the cause. That's the solution."

Once they had a plan, they wasted no time in implementing it. Richard was right, it did slow down their progress, but going around in circles was not really progress. Kahlan was glad that everyone seemed pleased by this new tactic. It also relieved the monotony of the long days of travel only to keep discovering that they weren't getting anywhere.

After they kept leapfrogging along their line for a number of days, Kahlan noticed that the terrain began to change. There were more rock outcroppings and they were larger, indicating that they were making it out of the strange woods. They eventually came to a small lake they had never seen before. After being in under the gloomy canopy for so long, they were all relieved to look out over the water and up at the open sky.

They dismounted by the shore to have a quick meal and a brief rest. Kahlan sat close to Richard. They were all relieved to simply be able look out at a new landscape as they ate some travel biscuits and dried meat.

Farther on, they came to some deadfall that again opened up the forest to the sky. The heavy clouds persisted, but at least the rain and mist had stopped.

The next morning, Richard took a deer with a clean shot with his bow. It took some time to skin and clean the deer, but they were all eager to give up a morning of travel in order to have some needed fresh meat. Travel biscuits and dried meat were getting old.

After riding for the rest of the afternoon and as darkness began to gather, they finally stopped to make camp for the night. Kahlan was more than relieved to finally be able to get down out of the saddle. She walked around a bit to get the circulation moving better in her legs.

Her pregnancy was beginning to make riding a horse uncomfortable.

As with every night so far, even though they were at last in a seemingly new place, there was no especially good defensive place to camp, so they had to again settle on a flat place among the trees. After picketing the horses and giving them some oats, they all trampled down the ferns and scraped the ground clear of forest debris to make spots for their bedrolls. There had been ample small streams for water whenever they made camp in the strange woods. Fortunately, now that the were out of those woods, all the recent rains meant that the streams were both plentiful and full.

"Why is it, do you suppose," Shale asked as she trampled some of the small plants, "that we came to that same rock again, with your mark on it, but we have never come across one of our campsites again? Doesn't that strike you as odd?"

Kahlan could tell that Richard's patience was wearing thin, and he had a time keeping his composure at the question.

"Your guess is as good as mine," he finally told her. "I need to collect wood."

The Mord-Sith noticed his quiet annoyance and busied themselves with clearing the ground for a place for the fire and collecting stones to make a fire ring. Kahlan knew they were all hungry, but no one said so. The mood was tense and none of them wanted to test Richard. For that matter, neither did Kahlan. She knew that something was bothering him.

Richard stacked wood for a fire over strips of birch bark and small sticks wiped on pine sap for kindling. He looked up at Shale and gestured. She knew what he meant and, with a flick of her hand, ignited a healthy flame in among the kindling. After the fire was burning hot he added new wood and after a time raked some of the glowing coals to the side and used them to cook some of the meat.

They used their knives to make long, sharp poles from young saplings in order to skewer and cook pieces of meat. Richard sliced off generous portions of the venison backstrap. It was the tenderest cut and everyone was eager to eat, but they merely said thanks when Richard handed each of them a piece and stuck them on their skewers. He set a number of chunks aside for anyone who wanted more. A few of the

Mord-Sith hardly charred the outside of their pieces before sinking their teeth into the meat. They all moaned with pleasure and rolled their eyes at the taste.

The meal did as much for everyone's spirits as it did for their stomachs.

31

"Thank you, Lord Rahl," Vika said, "for providing us this meal."

"Yes, thank you," Berdine added. "It's delicious!"

Between chewing, the rest of them chimed in with their thanks. Even Shale voiced her gratitude. Richard didn't say anything, but he did smile at them all, even if Kahlan thought it looked forced. Now that it seemed they were finally moving into new territory, no longer in the strange wood, and back on course, as well as having a good meal, everyone was feeling better.

"Although we've spent a great deal of time with you," Richard said to Shale without looking up, "we actually don't know much about you. Are your parents still alive?"

Kahlan instantly went on alert. His recent mood suddenly made sense to her. Although it was an innocent enough question, and no one else would have thought it was anything unusual, she recognized the subtle difference in Richard's tone of voice. That single question told her that Richard had asked that question not to make casual conversation, but as the Seeker.

It also told her that he knew the answer before asking the question. She didn't know what he was up to, but she knew she would find out soon enough.

Shale's gaze shifted uneasily among the rest of the group gathered close in around the warmth of the fire. The nights were getting colder and the wet chill seemed to go right to Kahlan's bones. The only real relief she got from shivering was when she could cuddle up against Richard during the nights.

"No," Shale finally answered. "My father passed a few years back." Her gaze drifted down to the flames. "My mother when I was younger."

Kahlan glanced around at all the faces watching the witch woman. "Mine too," she said into the uncomfortable silence. "My mother died when I was young. I know how terrible that is."

"Your mother was a witch woman, right?" Richard asked in a quiet voice, still without looking up. Again, Kahlan was aware that he already knew the answer, but for some reason he asked it anyway.

Shale nodded and devoted herself to pulling meat off with her teeth and then chewing. She clearly looked uneasy.

They all ate in silence for a short time.

"Tell me how your mother died," Richard said at last.

Kahlan glanced up. There it was.

She had been right about her instinct. This time, though, it was not a question, it was a command.

With their heads down, the Mord-Sith shifted their eyes among themselves. No one said a word. The death of a mother was not a pleasant subject for any of them, and not something they talked about. But they all recognized this as something different.

"What does it matter?" Shale finally said. "She's dead. That's all that really matters."

Richard didn't look up as he used a finger and thumb to pull a strip of meat from the chunk on the skewer.

"She was burned as a witch, wasn't she?"

Shale swallowed. "Lord Rahl . . ."

"Tell me what happened."

"Why do you wish to bring up such terrible memories?"

"Tell me what happened," he said in the same flat tone, still not looking up. The command in his words was clear, and Shale knew it.

Kahlan looked around at the Mord-Sith. They were all trying to look invisible. Except Berdine. She was watching attentively.

Kahlan reached over and put a hand on Shale's knee. "You are among friends. Sometimes it helps to talk about such things among those who care about you."

After a time, Shale finally let out a deep breath.

"All right." She leaned her skewer with a large chunk of meat ready to be eaten against a rock. "It was a harsh time in the Northern Waste. The crops had done poorly, so there weren't going to be enough reserves for the coming winter.

"The migration of the caribou had moved too far away that year for some reason, and the hunts were unsuccessful. The rains had swollen the rivers, and so catching salmon, the way we usually did, didn't go nearly as well as usual. Ducks and geese were nowhere to be found. Elk, bighorns, black bear, antelope, deer were all scarce. Even the rabbit population had been nearly wiped out by people desperate for food.

"It is said that such times come along every once in a while. The animals seem to know it will be an especially harsh winter, so they change their usual habits." She shrugged. "It is the way of nature. The animals for some reason pick a different route, a route they think will be better, or start sooner, and as a result the people in the place where I lived couldn't find enough meat or fish to salt or smoke for the winter.

"My father went to try to see what he could do to help. You know, go to other places to try to barter for meat, offer his services in return for supplies we badly needed. My mother was a healer, so she stayed to take care of people.

"My father had a hard time finding any kind of help anywhere close, as they were having similar troubles, so he had to travel farther. He was gone for a long time. So long that people thought he had left for good. People started to whisper that he had run away from my mother."

Shale stared off for a time before going on. "Rumors fed on themselves. Gossip led to yet more gossip, all the time getting wilder with ludicrous ideas."

"That's a dangerous stew," Richard said. "So then they started to say that it was all because of a witch woman in their midst?"

Shale smiled sadly. "Yes. They said that she drove all the animals far away. Other gossip said that her incantations and spells had deliberately driven the fowl and fish away." She looked up briefly. "My mother didn't do 'incantations,' but that made no difference to them. They said she did and so people believed it."

"Why would they think she would do that?" Berdine asked. "You know, chase the animals away. If she was a healer and helped them, why would they think she would do such a thing?"

Shale shrugged self-consciously as she rubbed her arms. "My mother had always cared for their needs. She was a kindhearted woman. Too kind. They began to see her kindness as somehow sinister. They said she was devious, hiding her cruelty behind a smile and her offers to help, when really, she intended them harm.

"As winter closed in, the rumors grew worse. They said that she had caused some of the new babies to be born dead, or their mothers to die in childbirth. They said that those things could only have been my mother's fault."

Kahlan slowly shook her head as she held the skewer over the fire, roasting another piece of meat. "Those aren't rare occurrences. Birth is a difficult process. Newborn babies don't always live, and mothers sometimes die in childbirth."

"True enough, but people refused to see it that way. Once they got it in their heads that it was a witch causing their troubles, there was no changing their minds. It was easy to blame her when there was no way to know the real cause. Soon, everything bad that happened had to be the witch's fault. There could be no other explanation, and none were sought or tolerated.

"My mother only had kindness in her heart and was horrified by the things they accused her of. She wept in despair. Her whole life, she had worked to show people that as a witch woman, she could be of help to them, that she could be a good part of their lives, that witch women needn't be feared. She always taught me that as witch women it was our duty to serve the needs of others, that we must devote ourselves to their betterment.

"She didn't believe it was necessary or much use to argue with people. Quarreling wasn't in her nature, and besides, she was aware that it would do no good. She had done good and expected her actions to be enough proof of her true nature. When she didn't wish to argue with people to deny the accusations, they somehow saw that as proof that she was guilty. When she finally did deny some of the more horrific accusations, they somehow saw that as proof of wackiness. Nothing my mother said would dissuade them of their beliefs."

She fell silent and stared into the flames, into the memories.

"So they burned her alive," Richard said.

Those words jolted Kahlan. This was where the Seeker had been headed. She just didn't yet know why.

Shale nodded as she continued to stare into the flames. After a moment she cleared her throat.

"There came an unexpected warm spell that lasted weeks. During that unusual weather people started coming down with a sickness they had never seen before. Some of the weaker people, old people, and infants died in delirium from the fevers. They wouldn't allow my mother to attend to the sick, saying that she was actually the cause of it. With every death, anger grew.

"In the middle of a dark night, they showed up and dragged my mother and me out of our home." Shale glanced up. "I was a witch woman, too, after all. I was being trained in the evil ways of a witch by my mother, they said. Everyone was yelling and screaming to kill the witches. I was terrified.

"My mother pleaded with them—calling most by name, as she had healed many of them at one time or another, saved many of their lives before, birthed their children—that she would admit to anything they wanted if they would simply leave me be.

"They were having none of it. They said both of us were witches and we both needed to burn.

"They threw me in a wood box, where firewood was stored, and nailed it shut to make sure I didn't get away until after they were finished with my mother and could come back for me. The sides had open slats for air circulation, so I could see out. Inside that dark box, crammed in atop the firewood, I watched what they did. I can still remember the smell of that firewood box.

"The men tied my mother to a long wooden rail and made her wait there on the cold, wet ground, helpless, as they built a huge, roaring fire in the center of town. The whole time she called them out by name, begging them to spare her daughter. That was all she cared about. While the men built the fire, women surrounded her, calling her names as they spit on her.

"And then three or four men lifted each end of the wooden rail and walked it over to the roaring fire. As everyone cheered, they heaved that rail with my mother tied helpless to it atop the blaze.

"In my dreams, I still hear her screams."

Shale stopped then, working to maintain her composure.

"Then, after my mother's screams finally stopped, they came for me. . . ."

Shale stopped there, and it seemed she might

not go on as she stared into the flames, seeing dark memories. Her face was stone.

"Then," she finally said, "I taught them why they should fear witches."

"How many of them did you kill?" Richard asked.

Shale shrugged. "I didn't keep a count. Once I broke out of that box, with my mother dead, I knew my life had changed forever. Her lessons of kindness had earned the hatred of people and gotten her murdered.

"I first took down the ones who had been guarding me to make sure I didn't escape. Once I started in on the rest, some managed to run and get away. But I knew who they all were. After I finished with those I caught near the fire, I hunted down every last person who had taken part in murdering my mother. I saw to it that not one of them had an easy death."

Richard tossed another stick of wood in the fire. "And so that is why you can't burn a witch, not even one as evil as Michec."

Shale nodded slowly as she stared into memories. "That is why."

"What happened when your father finally returned?" Kahlan asked.

Shale huffed. "What do you think happened? He was devastated. He didn't approve of what I had done, but he understood it. He was a hollow man after that. The life had gone out of him. His wife was dead and his daughter, the witch, had killed half the people in our town."

"What about everyone else after that?" Richard asked. "Not everyone took part in your mother's murder. And there were other people in the Northern Waste, other settled places. I presume you had to move, but you continued to live in the Waste."

Shale looked up at him, fire in her dark eyes. "After that, in the new places we moved to, I continued to help those in need. I healed people as my mother had taught me. I birthed babies. I attended the sick and did what I could when something could be done and comforted those for whom nothing could be done. I proved to people that I had a good side, a kind side.

"But from that day on, everyone in the Northern Waste knew the name Shale. What they hadn't realized when they burned my mother was that I was more than merely a witch woman, like my mother. I am also a sorceress, and that made me oh so much more dangerous.

"Needless to say, there were no more witch burnings. Those living in the Waste fear to even have that thought. Those in the Waste know that I am a witch in every sense, and more.

"They know that I don't live by their grace; they live by mine."

Bitterness soured Shale's expression. "You just don't understand what it is like to see your mother burned to death."

The witch woman stood, then, and walked off into the darkness.

32

Kahlan found Shale a short distance away, standing alone among a stand of birch trees, staring off into the darkness. She put a comforting hand on the witch woman's shoulder and gave it a gentle jostle.

"I'm sorry for all those terrible things that happened," Kahlan told her.

With her fingertips, Shale wiped a tear from under each eye. "Thank you. It's just that he doesn't understand what it's like to see your mother, a good woman who never harmed anyone, burned to death."

Kahlan leaned in and whispered. "Oh but he does."

Shale shook her head as she looked over at Kahlan. "How could he?"

Kahlan squeezed with the hand on Shale's shoulder. "When Richard was a boy their house burned down. His mother burned to death inside. Richard couldn't save her."

Shale clearly looked shocked. "I had no idea."

"As with you, it's not a story one is eager to tell."

"Then why did he want me to tell it?"

Kahlan pursed her lips, trying to think how to explain it when she herself wasn't yet entirely sure.

"This is about something more," she finally said. "When I first met Richard, Darken Rahl had invaded the Midlands. I came looking for the help of a Seeker. Richard's grandfather was a wizard, but Richard never knew it. His grandfather also happened to be the great wizard who had long been the caretaker of the Sword of Truth, an ancient weapon of great power.

"I urged Richard's grandfather to name a new Seeker. Because of the great need, he finally agreed. To my shock, he gave the sword to Richard and named him Seeker. Not because it was his choice, but, as he told me, because by Richard's actions and his life, he had revealed himself in a hundred little ways to be the one who had been born the true Seeker of Truth.

"That is how he came to have that ancient weapon and the title Seeker. The Sword of Truth is more than merely a weapon. It carries with it not only great power, but great responsibility that transcends the man alone. Only a true Seeker could understand that, and not use it merely to seek power for himself. That is how he came to be bonded to that singular blade.

"Richard always seeks to understand things, to seek answers. It's his nature, the way he was born, not something created in him by that weapon. The questions he asked you were not to hurt you, but because he needs answers to pieces of a larger puzzle.

"I don't know what that puzzle is—I often don't at first when he gets like this—but I do know we are all in grave danger and he sees something in the large picture about that danger that the rest of us don't see. He is seeking answers; he is not seeking to hurt you. You are part of that larger picture, and as such, part of the solution. He needs to know every facet of how you fit into it all.

"Richard knows very well that there are forces beyond life and death. Despite Michec being dead, Richard has concerns about the very real possibility of a threat of some kind, somehow surviving Michec's death. That is why he asked you to burn the witch man's body. He considered it essential.

"When you refused, that threw him off. It made no sense to him why you wouldn't do something that, in his mind, was so obviously necessary to ensure our safety. He is fighting—we are all fighting—against evil, and in that fight, there can be no quarter given, no mercy granted. He had to know why you refused so he can reassure himself that your reasons were sound.

"You just did that, and in so doing you showed us that you also fight evil, don't give quarter, and don't grant mercy to those who are undeserving."

It surprised Kahlan when Shale turned and gave her a hug. "Thank you, Mother Confessor, for explaining it to me in a way that I could understand, not the way he would have done it."

Kahlan smiled as they parted. "All of us—all nine of us—have lost our mothers when we were yet too young. The Mord-Sith all live with the horror of what was done to their mothers. Richard lives with the horror of his mother burning to death. My mother was lost to the horror of a terrible disease, but the loss hurts no less. We all lost our mothers and we all understand your pain. Never doubt that."

Shale nodded. "You are the Mother Confessor to us all, now."

Kahlan smiled. "Come on back and finish eating. You need your strength. We have a long and dangerous journey ahead of us. And, knowing Richard, he has more questions. Richard always has more questions. Sometimes it can be exasperating, but it never done out of malice."

As they walked together back through the birch stand and into the flickering firelight, everyone watched the two of them return, but were apparently reluctant to ask what had happened.

Shale rubbed her hands together, hesitating before saying anything. "I didn't finish my story," she finally told Richard in a much calmer tone as she offered him a smile. "Would you like me to tell you the rest?"

He returned the smile. "I'd like that."

Shale took a deep breath as she sat again and folded her legs. "Well, not everyone where we lived had been a part of that mob. Many hid in their houses, afraid to speak up against those filled with bloodlust, afraid to be accused along with my mother, afraid to be treated the same by people possessed by such fanaticism."

Richard shifted his legs to get more comfortable. "Human beings have an infinite capacity for ignorance and intolerance. As a result, they can be profoundly dangerous. Others rightly fear them."

"Indeed that's what happened," Shale said as she held her hands out before the fire to get them warm. "I treated the people of the Waste with help and kindness, just as my mother taught me, but only when they merited it. I didn't hold against the innocent the sins of the guilty. I treat each person for who they are. I treat evil people for what they are. It's as simple as that, and why I'm feared in the Northern Waste. Those who simply don't wish the help of a witch woman, I leave to themselves."

Richard smiled. "I, too, have met good people who didn't want anything to do with magic. That doesn't make them bad."

Shale couldn't help nodding at their shared experience with those who rejected or feared magic.

"News reached even the Northern Waste of the terrible things that had happened to the south of us. Fortunately, for the people there, we were far from the horrors of the war.

"From what I heard, though, I learned that you were one of those who fought against mindless brutality and hate, that as the Lord Rahl you fought that everyone might be able to live their own lives free of mindless persecution. While that was part of why I wanted to come here, there just seemed to be something more driving me to come."

"More?" he asked, looking up. "More, like what?"

Shale shrugged. "I don't know. Just an internal uneasiness, a nagging sense that I needed to come south. I'd like to think it's because after all that I learned about you and the Mother Confessor, I wanted to be a part of what you had created, to feel that my life and my abilities were worth something valuable to you, whereas they weren't by many others.

Also I felt I had to warn you and the Mother Confessor of the strange killings that, as we all learned later, turned out to be the Glee."

"We are glad you came, and we are in your debt for that and for so much more," Richard said in a soft, kind voice that somehow melted away the hard feelings of the questions.

"I know now, after the Mother Confessor spoke with me, that you are the Seeker. I didn't really know much about that before, or what it meant. I understand, now, that as the Seeker you are asking all these questions for a reason, not out of malice, even if I don't yet understand the reason. So, please go on and ask what you need to ask. I know now that you must have some deeper purpose."

Richard smiled as he handed her another piece of meat. "Berdine ate the piece you left."

"I thought she was done!" Berdine protested. "I didn't want it to go to waste, what with it already being cooked and all."

Shale let out a bit of a laugh as she took the meat and skewered it. "That's all right, Berdine. Easy enough to cook another. So what do you want to know about, Lord Rahl?"

"I want to know about the things Michec said just before he died."

As she held the chunk of meat on her skewer over the crackling flames, uncertainty colored her features. "He said something? I'm sorry, but I didn't hear him say anything. I was concentrating with all my strength, trying to hold back those vines he had around his wrists. He intended to also try to strangle you with them. Only by me holding them back was I able to stop him from conjuring more in order to do just that."

"Oh. Well, it's understandable that you were preoccupied."

"So, what did he say?"

"He said he was only following orders—the 'queen's' orders."

Shale frowned darkly at him from across the fire. "What queen?"

Richard shrugged. "I don't know. So then you have no idea, either?"

She pushed her dark hair back over her shoulder. "Not a clue."

"He also said, 'If you think this witch's oath begins and ends with me, you are a fool.'"

"Ah. I can see why that would be bothering you and why you wanted to know more about me." Creases tightened between her eyebrows. "But I thought it was his witch's oath that he was going to kill us."

"Apparently not. He said it didn't begin with him, and it wouldn't end with him. I think he was telling the truth."

"That is disturbing." She considered a moment. "What do you think it could mean?"

"I don't know." Richard looked up with that raptor gaze of his. "He said to ask you."

Shale looked startled. "Me! How should I know?"

Richard shrugged as he pulled off a strip of meat. "That's what he said. What do you know about witch's oaths?"

Shale rested her elbows on her knees as she thought it over. "I didn't know any witch women other than my mother. She never spoke of a witch's oath, as such. What do you think he meant?"

Richard shrugged. "From the way he put it, as if it was something quite solemn and serious, it sounded to me like he was saying that once a witch gives an oath, it is somehow the duty of every witch to see to it that such an oath is carried out."

Again, Shale looked surprised. "I can see why you were disturbed by the things he said. But I'm afraid I just don't know anything about such oaths." Her eyes narrowed with a memory. "Now that you mention it, though, my mother sometimes said that she had given an oath to help people, and that as a witch woman it was my duty to follow that oath. Out of respect for her, I often felt compelled to help people. Do you think that was what she meant? That it was a witch's duty to follow such an oath?"

"I'm afraid I don't know a whole lot about witch women," he said. "I was hoping you could fill in some of the blanks."

"Sorry. It's as puzzling to me as it is to you."

"Did you see the glint in his eye, after he was dead?"

She paused her chewing. "Glint? No, I saw no such thing."

"I did," Kahlan said, suddenly feeling alarmed.

Richard looked over at her. "You saw it too?" When she nodded, his brow drew down. "Then it wasn't my imagination."

"Maybe I was just too far away to see it," Shale suggested.

Richard fed another stick of wood into the fire. "Whatever it was, he is nothing but ashes, now."

Kahlan couldn't help wondering if such a witch's oath somehow lived on.

33

"Don't you think it's too early for me to be showing?" Kahlan asked the sorceress.

Shale glanced over from atop her horse. "There is no rule about such things. Different women start showing at different stages of a pregnancy. Some show much earlier than others."

"There was that strange wood," Cassia said from behind, "so it may actually not be as early as you think."

Kahlan cast a worried look back over her shoulder. "What do you mean?"

Cassia arced an eyebrow as she leaned forward in her saddle. "Tell me how long you think we were there, going in circles?"

Kahlan thought about it a moment. "I'm not sure."

"Exactly," Cassia said. "Last night when we made camp, I took stock of all of our supplies. I thought we should have plenty still left, but we've used up almost all of them while we were still in that strange, misty wood."

Kahlan stared back over her shoulder. "That seems unlikely."

"Check them yourself if you don't believe me. With as much as we took, they should have lasted us all the way to Aydindril, even going the long way. But they're almost all gone and we haven't yet even crossed the mountains."

When Kahlan thought about it, she realized that Richard had been having to find them a lot of food to supplement the travel supplies. She had thought that maybe it was because she had been eating as much as any three of them put together. But with the unborn babies, she seemed to need to eat a lot.

The deer meat was long gone. They had fortunately been able to catch a lot of fish, as well as rabbit, pheasant, a few turkeys, and even a big snake. Kahlan hadn't eaten any of that, though. Because of the food they had managed to catch along the way, they hadn't needed to rely solely on their traveling supplies, so Kahlan hadn't paid much attention to them.

Not only had they been catching a lot of the food they needed, but they had needed to spend considerable time to get that food. Fishing took time. Tracking animals took time. Hunting and cleaning their catches took time. Richard had taught all the Mord-Sith how to make snares for them to set at night, and while often successful, that took time as well.

"It can only mean that we were going in circles in those woods a lot longer than we thought," Cassia said.

Kahlan looked over at Shale. "What do you think?"

Shale sighed unhappily. "To tell you the truth, I've been wondering the same thing Cassia is wondering."

Kahlan didn't know what had gotten into the two of them. "You mean because of how big I am?"

"Yes, but it's more than that." Shale gave her a sidelong look. "I don't know how to put my finger on it, but there was something strange about those woods."

"Well, of course there was," Kahlan said. "We kept going around in circles."

"There's more to it than that alone." Before she went on, Shale leaned forward a little and patted her horse's neck when it began dancing around impatiently. "Now that we're out of there and at last into different country, hilly country with views of the mountains to the west and such, I realize that it wasn't just foggy in that forest. Thinking back on it, I realize now that my mind felt foggy as well.

"I don't know how to explain it, but my connection with my gift felt . . . different, somehow. I didn't even realize it until much later. I recognize now that I wasn't feeling myself back there or thinking clearly. I don't know exactly how to explain what I was feeling, but I guess I would say I felt disconnected from my gift. That may be why I didn't realize that there was a problem with those strange woods. Something was shrouding that sense."

Vale caught a red maple leaf as it drifted down and held it as she gestured around at the nearly bare tree branches and the decaying leaves on the ground. "And doesn't it seem too early to all of you for the leaves to have all fallen?"

Kahlan realized that the leaf Vale had caught was one of the last few colorful leaves that had hung on to the bitter end of the season. Most had long since fallen. The bare branches and the chilly bite to the air made her keenly aware of what had been making her vaguely uneasy. Somehow they had jumped right over autumn into early winter. The change to autumn came a little early up in the mountains, but they weren't yet up in the high country, and it wasn't changing to early autumn, it was already early winter.

"We had to have lost more time back in those woods than we thought," Shale said. "Somehow autumn vanished behind us and winter is already bearing down."

"It was a strange place," Rikka confirmed from behind. "I feel like I didn't really wake up until Lord Rahl got us out of there."

"Speaking of Lord Rahl," Nyda said, using the opportunity to walk her horse up closer, "what do you think could be taking him so long?"

Kahlan couldn't imagine. She had been trying not to worry about that very thing.

"He and Vika have been gone way too long," Berdine said. "I think we should go after him."

Kahlan hooked some of her long hair behind

an ear as she looked back. "He told us to wait here while he scouted ahead."

Berdine leaned forward in her saddle to gesture. "That's the other thing. Why would he do that? It doesn't make any sense. He is always saying that the nine of us have to stay together because of his magic law thing."

"The Law of Nines," Kahlan murmured. "But now that I think about it, it did seem like maybe he was looking a bit restless and distracted, like something was wrong." She turned back in her saddle to look at all the Mord-Sith in their red leather. "Did any of you pick up on that?"

After sharing blank looks, they all shook their heads.

"We don't know his small mannerisms nearly as well as you do," Nyda said. "You would be the first to recognize it if he was acting differently."

Kahlan idly rubbed her palm on the saddle's horn as she started to remember the odd little signals that told her something was bothering him. She hadn't put them together at the time. She should have.

"Now that I think about it, why wouldn't he tell us all we could go ahead and dismount, if he was planning to be gone this long?" That was one more thing that confirmed to her that she had good reason to worry.

"Do you want to go look for him?" the sorceress asked.

Kahlan thought it over briefly, finally forcing out an unhappy breath. "No. The woods in this area are pretty dense. There are low spots with bogs making it a maze to get through. We don't know the route Richard took. He knows where we are and how to find us as long as we stay here. We shouldn't take the chance on going a different way and getting separated."

Too troubled to sit still any longer, she swung her leg over the back of her horse to get down. "But I'm tired of sitting in the saddle."

The rest of them agreed with her sentiment and were happy to dismount. After staring off into the distant woods for a while longer, Kahlan tied the reins of her horse to a branch so she could pace. A few of the others sat on a nearby outcropping of granite ledge covered with colorful splotches of lichen, and a couple of the others on a log. Kahlan saw a squirrel, up on a branch, chirping down at them to get out of its territory.

As she paced, she had a sudden thought.

"When we were in that wood, do any of you remember seeing any animals?"

Shale thought it over briefly. "No, as a matter of fact, I can't say that I do. But now, when I try to remember that strange wood, for some reason, the memory of the place seems dim and distant, like a dream you forget later on."

Cassia snapped her fingers. "That's it, exactly. That's how I feel thinking back on it. Like it was a dream. Now that I think about it, I can't even say that we were really there."

The others agreed about that part of it. None of them, though, could remember ever seeing any wildlife.

Kahlan looked up at the bare bark of the maple trees. To the right, a breeze rattled the exposed branches of the birches. As she stared around at the thinning trees, she ran her hand over the swell of her belly.

She unexpectedly began to worry about how long they had actually been there in those woods, traveling around in big circles. It made her apprehensive to realize that she could be a lot farther along in her pregnancy than she thought. If that was true, how was she to judge when the babies would be due?

"There were no birds," she said at last, picturing the place in her mind. "I remember thinking at the time that it was strange that I didn't see any birds." She looked over at the others. "Anyone remember seeing birds there?"

No one did.

They sat around, or paced, for what had to be several more hours, growing more edgy the whole time. Picking at the reindeer moss on the rough trunk of an oak tree, Kahlan glanced up and saw the sun sinking low in the sky. Like time itself, the day was slipping away on them. She worried that Richard wasn't back.

As she was flicking a piece of moss off the tree, Kahlan heard something. She rushed forward a few steps, peering into the distance. Everyone looked expectantly toward the noise off in the shadows. They were all relieved when they saw Richard and Vika on their horses riding back into view among young pines.

As soon as they reached Kahlan and the small group, rather than apologizing for how long it had taken them, Richard and Vika hurriedly jumped down off their horses.

"We have a problem," Richard said without any greeting.

Kahlan looked from Richard's face to Vika. Both of them were sweaty and looked pale.

"What is it?" Kahlan stepped closer and gripped his forearm. "What happened?"

As they all came closer to gather around Kahlan, Richard ran his fingers back through his hair as he tried to think of a way to explain it.

"We ran into the boundary."

Kahlan squinted as she leaned in toward him. "The boundary? What boundary?"

He gestured irritably back over his shoulder. "The boundary. You know, the boundary." Then he gestured off at the mountains to the west. "Remember the boundary that used to run down those mountains between D'Hara and the Midlands? Like the boundary that was between the Midlands and Westland—the one you came through with Shar. That boundary."

"Who is Shar?" the sorceress asked.

Kahlan flicked her hand and shushed the woman.

She was having difficulty in her own mind making sense of what he was saying. He was pretty upset. She thought he had to mean something else and she just wasn't understanding him.

"What did it look like?"

Richard threw up his hand. "You know what the boundary looks like, Kahlan! As you get close it becomes a big green wall. The closer you get, you start melting into it, the green grows stronger and then turns dark. The voices on the other side start to call to you. You start seeing their faces—faces of people you know, people calling you by name."

Kahlan looked over at Vika's ashen face. "You saw the same thing?"

The Mord-Sith swallowed. "When we got close enough, the surroundings disappeared as everything turned dark. My mother called to me from the other side of that dark wall. I saw her." Her eyes welled with tears. "She reached out for me." Vika swallowed back the tears again. "I tried to go to her. Lord Rahl pulled me back just in time, or I would have been lost."

Shale looked exasperated. "What in the world are you people talking about? What in the name of Creation is a boundary?"

"It's nothing from Creation." Richard took a breath, trying to regain his patience so he could explain it. "Think of it as a kind of fracture in the world of life. It lies like a curtain across the land. That curtain is death itself in this world.

If you were to walk far enough into it, it's like walking off the edge of a cliff and falling into the underworld."

The sorceress stammered as if such a thing were unreasonable. "But what if someone comes along and walks into it without knowing what it is?"

Richard leaned toward her. "Then they die, right then and there."

Shale's gaze shifted about uneasily, as if she was searching for some kind of answer that made sense to her. "Well, how long is this curtain of death? Can't we simply ride around the end of it?"

Kahlan could see the muscles in Richard's jaw flex as he gritted his teeth.

"That's why it took Vika and me so long to get back," he finally said. "We rode a long way in each direction trying to see if it ends somewhere. It doesn't. If you go to the right, it goes straight west. To the left it starts hooking back up this way as it goes to the northeast."

"Could we all go farther than you were able to go and find an end, do you think?" Kahlan asked.

Richard gave her a look she understood all

too well. "Could we have done that with the boundaries before? The ones between our lands? Could we have gotten around it that way? Their nature is to be a boundary, to restrict passage, so while I can't say for sure, but knowing what the boundary from before was like, it isn't likely that it has an end we could simply travel around. It completely blocks us from our plan of going south to get around the worst of the mountains."

Kahlan searched around for a solution. "Can't you find us a way through, like you did before?"

Richard had obviously already considered that and had an answer ready. "That boundary was failing. This one isn't. It's much more powerful than the last one I saw. We aren't going to be able to get through it."

"Then what are we going to do?" Kahlan asked, feeling a rising sense of panic at the thought of having her children exposed, out in the middle of nowhere.

The Glee were likely to be somewhere behind, looking for them. They needed to get to the safety of the Keep before they found her and the twins. Every moment they were out in the open increased the danger.

Richard averted his eyes and reluctantly gestured to the west. “We have no choice but to go west, directly over that imposing mountain range. We have no choice.”

“Well,” she finally said, trying to find a reason for optimism, “if we can find a way over the mountains, that would be a shorter route to get to Aydindril.”

The sorceress wasn’t about to be placated. “Show me this boundary thing.”

34

Richard reined in his horse and pulled it sideways to block the others. "It's too dangerous to ride our horses any farther," he told them. "We need to get off here and go the rest of the way in on foot."

Once they had handed the reins of their horses to the Mord-Sith, he told them that he wanted them all to wait where they were and take care of the horses. They weren't happy about leaving Richard and Kahlan without their protection, but because it involved dangerous magic, they were happy to keep their distance. Only Vika insisted on coming with them. Richard agreed with a nod.

Richard led Shale, Kahlan, and Vika on foot forward through an eerie stand of dead spruce. The silver-gray skeletons stood in dried, cracked, black ground that had once been thick mud. The grove of spruce were devoid of all but a few stubby, bare branches draped with long trailers of dull green moss that hung motionless in the dead-still air. The place smelled as dead as it looked. Kahlan walked behind with Vika, gazing warily around at the dead trees.

The ground descended gradually into a wet area growing thick with bog weed that now had died off until next spring. The long reeds around the open water had previously been blown over by heavy gusts of wind and were likewise brown and dead. It was difficult to slog their way through the tangled mat. Small, unseen things darted away in the murky water.

Bugs buzzed around their heads. Kahlan had to use her fingernails to pull out biting flies crawling on her neck under her hair. From time to time Richard and Vika tried to swish the cloud of insects away. It did little good. They all swatted at the flies that bit them. Shale held her dark cloak tightly closed against the insects. That morning there had already been a frost, so she knew that while the bugs were a nuisance, they would all soon be gone with the first hard freeze.

Kahlan didn't hear any other sounds, but she kept looking around for anything unexpected. She was sure the place had to be full of snakes so she was careful of where she stepped.

As they came up through thick grasses onto higher ground, Richard lifted a hand to bring them all to a halt.

"This is the place."

"This is what you're worried about?" Shale looked off in both directions. "I don't see anything."

"Stay where you are and watch," he said.

He walked forward cautiously. As he did, Kahlan could see a green glow, at first hardly perceptible, form around him. It grew brighter in the area immediately around him until after a few more steps it brightened to a sheet of glowing green light that looked like it was pressing in around him. The ominous, wavy, distorted green wall grew larger with every step he took. The green light was stronger close to him and faded away to the sides and above.

Kahlan was able to see the forest and sky beyond the lighter portion of the wavering green light. As Richard finally turned and walked back to them, the green glow faded until he was far enough away, where it vanished completely.

Kahlan folded her arms, feeling a little sick at seeing such a thing again. She never thought she would. She did her best to force the terrible memories it brought back from her mind.

"What does it feel like when you get close like that?" Shale asked in a low voice, finally concerned. "I don't see why you say it's an opening to the underworld. I admit, it's strange-enough-looking, but it doesn't look like a wall of death, as you described it to us. It's just that unusual green light."

"You would know why if you got close to it," Vika told her.

Shale stared at the Mord-Sith a moment, then turned back to Richard. "I need to get closer. I need to be as close as possible if I'm to try to sense the nature of its magic."

Richard nodded his agreement. "Now that I've shown you that much of its characteristics, I'll take you in so you can see it and feel it for yourself." He gestured to Vika. "Why don't you wait here."

The Mord-Sith nodded. "Seeing it once is enough for me."

Shale didn't look the least bit reluctant to see what didn't look all that frightening from where they were. When Richard started out, Kahlan, knowing what was coming, walked beside Shale.

"Easy, now," Richard said as he finally locked arms with the sorceress.

"What are you doing?" she asked.

"Just keep hold of my arm. I'll stop you when we've gone far enough."

"What do you mean, when we've gone far enough?"

Despite her reluctance, Kahlan locked her arm with Shale's other arm. "It's best if you let us hold on to you. You'll see."

As they walked closer and a faint green glow began, it was different-looking than when they had watched from the outside as Richard walked close by himself. It almost felt like it was humming. Shale looked up and then to the sides.

As they went farther in, Kahlan started hearing that awful, high-pitched buzzing sound, like a thousand bumblebees. With each step, the sound became not only louder but deeper in tone. Kahlan knew, though, what the sound actually was. That knowledge ran a shiver up her spine.

As they continued in, the green light deepened in color. The woods all around became darker, too, as if it were twilight.

Abruptly, an entire sheet of green materialized, the greenish glow everywhere around them. Kahlan looked back. She could no longer see the others. The woods and everything beyond had been swallowed in darkness. The cloud of insects dispersed rather than go any farther in.

"Easy," Richard warned them as he stepped carefully.

After a few more steps, the green vanished as the whole world darkened to black. It felt like a moonless, starless night, where she couldn't see her hand in front of her face. The buzzing vibrating deep in Kahlan's chest was so strong that it was starting to make her feel sick to her stomach.

She put a hand over her babies, suddenly worried, wondering if it was a mistake to take them close to such an evil place.

The darkness abruptly became a distinct, darkly transparent wall, like looking out on a night through glass that had grease smeared all over it. Kahlan could see the shapes moving beyond.

"This is as far as we dare go," Richard said.

Kahlan realized that she was putting pressure on Shale's arm to draw her back. She eased up on the pressure to let her go farther forward. The sorceress needed to know what they were really facing. They had to let her get a little closer.

Shale's jaw fell open as inky black shapes swept by, close, in the gloom on the other side of that dark wall. Kahlan knew they were specters in the deep, the dead in their lair. The swirl of inky shapes was at first bewitching, but Kahlan knew better.

She felt overwhelmed by the darkness and then began to feel that old sense of longing for what lay beyond. She heard voices murmur her name, calling to her. Kahlan knew they would be calling to Richard by name. By the way that Shale's eyes opened wider, she knew they were calling to her by name as well. Those thousands of distant voices of the souls beyond were the buzzing they had heard at first. Now, each of those sounds resolved into uncountable individual voices, the appeals of the dead.

When Shale cried out and tried to lift her arms toward the dark wall, Richard and Kahlan had to forcefully pull her arms back. She let out a long, mournful wail. As they pulled the sorceress back, she struggled to reach out toward the dead, to get to them, trying to tear herself out of Richard's and Kahlan's arms. As they dragged her back, she dug in her heels, not wanting to be pulled away from what she saw.

When they were far enough back, Shale sagged in their arms, weeping. Knowing the agony of what she had seen, Kahlan felt a pang of sadness for her. She wished they hadn't had to show it to her, but she needed to see it to truly understand. Richard and Kahlan had to continue struggling, pulling the sorceress back away from the wall of death.

When they were far enough back, to where Vika waited, Shale finally grasped the magnitude of what she had seen and reacted in horror to what she had tried to do. As she fell to tears, Kahlan took the sorceress in her arms.

"Think of something else," Kahlan told her. "Shale, listen to me. You have to think of something else. Try to remember every town you passed through on your way to come to the

People's Palace. Think. Try to remember them in order."

After a few moments Shale pushed back and swallowed. "I'm all right."

Hooking her arm through Shale's to be safe, Kahlan ushered her back away until they reached the others.

She finally stood on her own, wiping tears from her cheeks. "I've never in my life felt magic that powerful."

"It's not something pleasant, that's for sure," Richard said. "I have absolutely no idea why it's here. All I can tell you is that it shouldn't be. As far as I know, there is no one powerful enough to call up that boundary. I'm sorry for what you saw in there, but I felt that you needed to see it, feel it, for yourself."

Shale stared in wonder at him. She looked too stunned to speak. Kahlan knew, though, that it wasn't the world of the dead that had her looking so shocked. It was something else.

The sorceress abruptly reached out and put fingers to Richard's temples. "Hold still."

Richard turned a worried glance toward Kahlan, as if to ask what to do.

"Do as she asks," Kahlan said. "Hold still."

From not far away, the Mord-Sith, looking in ill humor, all watched. They didn't particularly like anyone but Kahlan touching Lord Rahl. It aroused their protective instincts. Kahlan held a hand out low in their direction, letting them know it was all right and to stand down.

All at once, Shale drew both hands back with a gasp, as if the touch had burned her fingers. She took a step back away from Richard, clearly in fear.

Kahlan was alarmed by her reaction. "What is it?"

Shale's terrified eyes looked from Kahlan back to Richard.

"Shale," Kahlan asked again, "what is it that you sense?"

Shale blinked at her. "It's him."

Both Richard and Kahlan shared a bewildered look.

"What are you talking about?" Kahlan asked. "What's him?"

Shale gathered her long, dark hair together and held it in both fists. She drew her lower lip through her teeth.

Her face had gone ashen. "It's his."

Growing impatient, Kahlan made a face.

"His what?"

She hesitated. "The boundary. It's Lord Rahl's magic."

Richard closed the distance to the sorceress and grabbed her by an arm. "What are you talking about?"

"You created this, this . . ." She waggled a hand toward where they had just been. ". . . this boundary. This fracture in the world of life. This opening into the world of death. It's your magic that created it. I can feel it. I can feel your gift in its composition. You did this."

35

Richard gritted his teeth as he tightened his grip on her arm. "What are you talking about? What do you mean I'm doing it?"

Shale swallowed at the fire in his eyes. "As a sorceress I can sense a person's individual gift, much the way you can recognize a person by their voice, or their eyes. Your gift, like everyone's gift, has a unique feel to it, except yours is more recognizable and distinctive to me than most. The gift that empowers that wall of death, that boundary as you call it, is your gift."

Richard stared at her for the longest time. "That's impossible. I don't have any idea how to create such a thing," he finally said.

Shale pulled her arm back. "I didn't say you did. But the feel of your gift is unmistakable to me. It is your gift that brought up that boundary wall."

Richard growled in frustration. "It can't be. I would have no idea how to do such a thing."

"It's in your blood," Kahlan told him.

They all turned to her. "Your grandfather created the original boundaries," she explained. "He's the only one who could have. The awareness of the organic process involved with using his gift to create the boundaries must have somehow, in some way, been passed on to you along with his gift. You are a powerful and gifted war wizard, in many ways one of the most talented ever to live. Although you have never created a boundary before, the ability to do so is surely inborn in you."

Richard pinched the bridge of his nose, trying to get a grip on the anger clearly boiling right at the surface. His head finally came up and he tried hard to maintain his composure.

"All right, let's say that I have the inherent ability. Fine. But I didn't do it. I would know if I used my gift to create something this profound."

"I think that has to be true," Shale agreed. "But that means that someone else used your gift to pull up that curtain of death across our path."

He stared at her for a long moment. "If I didn't do it, then who could have?"

Shale looked at a loss to explain it. "I'm sorry, Lord Rahl, but until now, if I hadn't felt it myself—with my own gift—I would never have imagined such a thing was even possible. But then again, having been raised in the Northern Waste, my knowledge of the gift and all its capabilities is limited to what I learned from my father and mother. All I can say is that it has to be that someone powerful is usurping your gift.

"I can only imagine that it would take great power to do such a thing. You said there is no longer anyone powerful enough to do such a thing. But you told me before that gifted people can join their abilities together in order to do what none of them could do alone. Remember?"

His fists on his hips, he nodded. He stared at the sorceress for a time, his sense of reason finally rising up through his anger. He cooled considerably.

"That has to be the explanation. It has to be gifted people joining their power to be able to do this. That means that we're likely not dealing with a single gifted person, but a group of them."

"One gifted person, or a group, it has been done." Kahlan spread her arms in frustration. "Either way, at this point the more relevant question is *why* would they do such a thing?"

"If they wanted to kill us, it's highly unlikely that those powerful enough to do such a thing would think we would be foolish enough to simply walk into the boundary and be killed." The calm demeanor of the Seeker was back. "The strange wood wasn't life-threatening, it simply slowed us down. The boundary they put up must also be meant to stop us, not kill us. After all, stopping people from passing was the purpose of the boundaries."

"But why?" Kahlan asked.

He paced off a ways, then turned and came back with a look that worried her. "I think they don't want us getting away with the twins. I think their purpose is to keep us from going to the Keep where the twins would be safe."

Kahlan looked off toward the new boundary. "That's a frightening thought."

Richard let out a sigh of resignation. He held up a hand as he thought out loud.

"We can't get through that boundary to get any farther to the southwest in order to go around the mountains, so at this point our only two choices are to either go back to the People's Palace or try to get to Aydindril by going straight northwest over the mountains. Back toward the palace, we will be attacked relentlessly by the Glee. They are determined to slaughter us. If we try to get to Aydindril by trying to get over those mountains, I can only assume we will encounter those who are doing all of this."

Kahlan felt a rising sense of panic. "They want the babies."

"We all will protect the twins," Shale said.

With one hand on a hip, Richard rubbed his forehead with the fingertips of his other hand as he paced off a ways before finally returning to look at Shale.

"If it's my gift doing this, then is there a way for you to . . . to, I don't know, cut my gift off from it so that the boundary will lose its viability and come down?"

Shale looked off toward the boundary, as if she could still see it and hear the call of the dead.

"I suspect that now that it's up, it no longer needs your magic to persist. Once it's up, it's up. After all, once your grandfather used his gift to create the ones before, they were there and they didn't then need his gift to continue to exist, did they?"

"No," he admitted. He let out a sigh. "What matters is that someone doesn't want us to go south to take the twins out of reach." He gestured toward the mountains. "We have nowhere else to go except that way."

"Then it's surely a trap," Vika said as she stepped forward, unable to remain silent any longer. "We shouldn't indulge them and walk into their trap. Especially since they have already proven that they have enough power that they can use your gift."

Richard gave her a curious look. "Since when have the Mord-Sith not wanted to run headlong into trouble?"

"If it was me, and the others, we would do so in a heartbeat and without a second's thought." Vika gestured at Kahlan. "But the Mother Confessor carries the children of D'Hara and our hope for the future. It is for her that I am reluctant to take the risk."

"Well," he said, wiping a weary hand over his face, seeming a little surprised at how much sense she was making, "whoever used my gift has to be off that way. We don't know what other unexpected things they might do if we don't find them and stop them. Better on our terms than theirs."

Kahlan felt trapped by the unknown. "But they obviously want us to try just that so they can get our children."

Richard looked sympathetic but determined. "All the more reason we must find them and put a stop to it. The only way to protect the twins is to stop whoever is doing this, or just like the Glee, they will come after us in another way when we least expect it."

Despite the terror of the implications, Kahlan knew he was right. She tried to sound positive. "I guess if we can stop this threat and, in the process, find a way over the mountains, we will end up much closer to Aydindril and we will reach the Keep all that much sooner."

Richard smiled. "That's what I'm hoping." He gestured to the mountains. "The threat is that way. There are nine of us, so we have the Law of Nines on our side. The sooner we find and eliminate the threat, the better. With winter closing in those mountains will become even more treacherous. We need to get over them before the worst of it sets in. We can still make some distance before we need to make camp for the night so I think we should press on."

He looked around at all the faces watching them. "Just be aware that going through those mountains will be difficult and dangerous even if we can beat the weather, and even without the threat that's out there."

Everyone gave him a grim nod.

With the decision made, everyone mounted up.

As soon as they started out, Kahlan rode up close to Richard so the others wouldn't hear her. "I can tell by that 'Seeker look' in your eyes that you might know who could be waiting for us in that trap up there in those forbidding mountains."

He rode in silence for a time before he gave her an unreadable look. "I have a nasty suspicion, but I'm not ready to say it out loud, yet."

"Richard Cypher," she admonished in the name she knew him by when she first came to know him and fall in love with him, a name that touched on deep history and meaning for them both, "don't give me that. Tell me what you're thinking."

He gave her a look for using that name and then rode on for a time before answering. "I think we're making it too complex. I think it all boils down to one simple question."

Kahlan stared over at him as she swayed in her saddle. "What question?"

"When he was dying, Michec said that the witch's oath didn't begin and end with him. So who, then?"

Kahlan felt an icy jolt of realization wash through her veins.

"Shota."

36

As they followed the natural lay of the land to begin the ascent up into the mountains to try to find a pass, the forest thinned as it struggled to grow among the granite ledges and masses of rock that rose up all around. The exposed rock was covered in colorful medallions of lichen. Fluffy moss and small plants with deep green, heart-shaped leaves grew in low clefts in the ledges.

In the more rocky places, scraggly trees struggled to hold on to the rock with roots like claws. The roots grew in fat, twisting clusters over and around walls of stone and down over granite that looked like disorderly stacks of giant blocks. Ferns found a home in the crooks of those roots, and in the ferns, dirt collected to allow spotted mushrooms and other small plants to grow. Thin trailers of vines hung down from small ledges in the stone. Where water seeped down sheets of sloped granite, green slime grew, and in the laps of rock that collected the water small, colorful frogs waited for bugs.

Squirrels in the upper branches followed the progress of the invaders, chattering warnings as they leaped from branch to branch. Mockingbirds flitted about, or called out as they flicked their long tails. Richard saw ravens perched on branches high up in the larger spruce trees, watching them pass below. When they took to wing, the massive trees left plenty of space for them under the canopy to swoop through the forest. They sent out loud calls as they soared among the trees.

Richard heard a strange moan from Kahlan. He slowed and turned in his saddle.

"What's wrong?"

Kahlan doubled over. "I think I'm going to be sick."

He leaped off his horse when he saw her start to slump to the side and begin to slide off her saddle. He rushed in under her just in time to catch her fall enough to ease her limp form to the ground. The others all jumped off their horses when they saw her go down.

Kahlan crossed her arms over her middle as she let out a groan of agony. As Richard brushed her hair back from her face so he could see her eyes, he saw that she was covered in sweat. Her pupils were dilated. She looked up at him with panic in those green eyes.

"What's wrong?"

She clutched his sleeve, pulling herself up toward him, and opened her mouth, but she couldn't bring forth words before the pain overwhelmed her and her arm went slack. Her eyes rolled up in her head as she sagged back to the ground.

He put a hand to the side of her face and called her name again. He didn't think she had even heard him that time.

Shale rushed in and urgently dropped to the ground on the other side of Kahlan. The sorceress took one look at Kahlan's ashen face and immediately started unbuttoning her shirt stretched tight over her round belly.

"Loosen her trousers," she told Richard. After a quick look, she said, "Get them off. She's bleeding."

Richard felt numb. He did as the sorceress asked and then sat back on his heels. He didn't know what to do. He had never felt so afraid and helpless.

Shale placed the flats of her hands on the sides of Kahlan's belly, then on the top and near the bottom. She lifted Kahlan's eyelids, looking into her eyes. She put an ear to Kahlan's chest and listened to her heart and her breathing.

She looked up at last, her expression grim.

"She's miscarrying."

Richard blinked, the words seeming to come at him from some faraway place.

"What?"

"She's losing the babies."

"She can't," he said.

Shale looked up at him with as bleak an expression as he'd ever seen. "If we don't act quickly, we are going to lose her as well."

Richard sat frozen in terror, his skin feeling icy cold with goose bumps. He couldn't lose her. She couldn't lose her children.

Shale placed one hand on Kahlan's belly and the other on her forehead. She muttered a curse under her breath.

Richard looked up at the Mord-Sith all

standing around them, as if to implore their help. They looked as alarmed and lost as he felt.

Kahlan groaned again as she folded both arms across her middle and sat halfway up with the cramping pain that made her cry out. She muttered something incoherently.

Shale put an arm under Kahlan's head and helped her ease back down. Vale rushed to her horse and quickly returned. She reached in to hand the sorceress a folded blanket. Shale put it under Kahlan's head. Someone gave Richard another blanket, which he laid over Kahlan's bare legs. Sweat was pouring off her face despite the chilly air.

"But she will be all right," Richard insisted.

Ignoring his words, Shale finally sat back up on her heels. "I need you to do something."

"Anything. Name it."

"I need you to get me some mother's breath."

Richard's mind felt blank. "Mother's breath?"

Shale glanced up, giving him a look as if to say she didn't have time for questions. "Yes, it's a plant with leaves that—"

"I know what it is," Vika said. "I grew up in mountainous country. That's where mother's breath grows—in the high country."

Richard looked around frantically. "Would there be any around here?"

Vika took a worried look over her shoulder at the mountains towering above them. She pointed.

"It grows much higher up, near the tree line. There is already snow in a lot of places up there. Mother's breath dies out when the snows come."

Richard shot to his feet, snatching up the reins to his horse. "We need to get up there and find some."

Shale looked up at them both. "I need the whole plant, roots and all."

Vika cast a troubled look up the mountain. "It's liable to be covered in snow by now. Snow kills off mother's breath until it comes back in the spring."

Shale shook her head vehemently. "It can't be dead and dry. If it's not still living and supple it turns to a poison that would kill her."

"It's an extremely rare plant." Vika hesitated. "I've only seen it a few times in my whole life. It doesn't grow in many places. What if we can't find any?"

Shale gave them both a look. "She's losing

the babies. I don't know if I can save her. Go find the mother's breath. It's her only chance, now."

"What about the twins?" Richard asked.

Shale pointedly wouldn't look up at him. "Go. Hurry."

Richard and Vika shared a look; then each stuffed a foot in a stirrup and leaped up into their saddles.

"The rest of you," Richard said, gesturing to the Mord-Sith, "watch over them until we're back."

He looked down at Kahlan. Her eyes were half closed. She trembled in pain. She truly did look like she was dying. Richard swallowed and gestured to Vika.

"Let's go."

The story continues.

Episode 5 of the Children of D'Hara

INTO DARKNESS

coming soon...